Bella Mia

Published by Calisi Press in the United Kingdom 2015
Calisi Press, Folkestone CT19 4NW
www.calisipress.com
info@calisipress.com
ISBN 978-0-9932380-2-4

First published under the original title:
BELLA MIA
by Elliot Edizioni, Rome 2014
Copyright © 2014 Elliot Edizioni s.r.l.

Translation Copyright © Franca Scurti Simpson, 2016
Edited by Marinella Mezzanotte

Cover and book design by:
Charlotte Mouncey, Bookstyle (http://www.bookstyle.co.uk)
Printed and bound in Great Britain by Clays Ltd, St Ives plc

To Piera and Anna Rita, to their children

Once upon a time I was very light, I weighed a few kilos. Once upon a time there were only three or four kilos of me, only a few kilos of me, only a few kilos had my name.
MARIANGELA GUALTIERI, Fuoco centrale (2003)

PREFACE

In the small hours of the 6th April 2009 an earthquake of 6.3 magnitude on the Richter scale struck Italy, with the city of L'Aquila in the central Abruzzo region at its epicentre. The tremor lasted for 20 seconds. Italy has a long history of earthquakes: in 1703 L'Aquila was decimated by a major tremor that killed 5,000 people. In April 2009, more than 300 died, over 1,500 were injured and around 65,000 had to leave their homes. It was the deadliest earthquake in Italy since 1980, when more than 2,500 people were killed near Naples.

Despite months of foreshocks leading up to April 2009, many in L'Aquila had chosen to stay in their homes after receiving assurances from the Italian National Commission for the Forecast and Prevention of Major Risks. Laws had been introduced after the 1980 catastrophe, obliging construction to be carried out according to anti-earthquake standards, with politics and corruption often blamed for the poor enforcement of these laws.

This story takes place in the aftermath of the 2009 earthquake, when the homeless have been housed in temporary accommodation while awaiting reconstruction, some in prefabs known as M.A.P. (*Modulo Abitativo Provvisorio*, Temporary Residential Unit, also used as classrooms in schools), others in the C.A.S.E. (*Complessi Antisismici Sostenibili ed Ecocompatibili* – Sustainable and eco-compatible earthquake-proof housing complexes). Other temporary buildings mentioned in the text are

M.U.S.P. (*Modulo ad Uso Scolastico Provvisorio* – Temporary School Modules).

The C.A.S.E. project consists of 185 buildings in 19 locations, a total of 4,500 flats housing over 15,000 people. The blocks of furnished flats, over two or three storeys, were built on earthquake-proof 'platforms', resting on pillars designed to isolate the buildings from the ground in the event of another earthquake. The acronym spells the Italian word for 'homes'.

1

He sits in his place, a shaggy head hanging over the bowl. The steam from the soup enlarges the pores of his spotty skin and curls the long, thin hairs sprouting aimlessly, not yet planning to become a beard. From the noise of his cutlery you'd think he's working hard, but he eats very little. He pushes his food around for a long time, but the spoon going to his mouth is almost empty. He avoids our eyes, he knows that we are looking at him and counting the calories ingested and those left on the plate.

He chews on his own silence.

I can't quite love this boy, not completely. Tall, skinny, a body made of broken lines, with no curves, an unexpected fragility in the outline of his legs just under the knee. His grandmother still treats him like a little boy; as for me, I don't know how to approach him. He's an adolescent, he seems younger sometimes.

I felt an easy tenderness for him when he was a little boy with dark curls and a heart-shaped little mouth; he had plenty of the grace needed by the young to ensure the preservation of the species, back then. I would bombard him with kisses on those weary afternoons he was left with me. He used to smell like a puppy, now he leaves a trail of stale armpit and unwashed hair sometimes, as he goes by without a sound. With his T-shirt off, he's a landscape of protruding ribs on one side, and vertebrae on the other. He stoops, in the posture of someone who has just stopped, with his belly, a ball kicked hard at him. I don't always recognise him at a distance, from the back. He has grown so quickly.

We find ourselves around this reconstructed table that belongs to none of us. We all used to have our own: the widowed grandmother in her village house, me in the centre of town, and him, with his mother, not far away. The two of them had been back a year and a half, when it happened. Now we're together, the three of us alone in the flat we have been assigned. He is ours, my nephew, my mother's grandson.

We didn't need the earthquake, we already had our own tribulations. But my sister had been happy to come back with her son. An acceptable compromise, she used to say. She had found her way back to old places, suspended friendships, a slower pace of life. It had quickly softened the separation.

On Sunday afternoons in winter we'd find each other having coffee at our mother's place, sitting under the low-hanging light in the dining room. She spoiled us, a little chocolate materialising, as if by chance, next to the steaming cup. Later there would be a bowl of fruit peeled by invisible hands, and the excuse of having to pick up the laundry from the line in the yard to facilitate confidences between the two of us.

When he was not out with friends he'd come along, headphones on. He'd leave us on the outside. He does the same some mornings now, if he misses the bus and I drive him in. He turns the music pouring into his ears into a barbed-wire fence between me and him. At those times perhaps he feels more vulnerable, more careful of protecting his distance. He holds himself inside his coat, pulls up the collar, uses the cloth as a barrier and makes himself unreachable. He looks stubbornly out of the window, or at the hem of his trousers and his shoes. He holds on so tight to avoid being thrown against me on a right turn, that his knuckles go white. When we turn the other way, he flattens himself against the glass, his face and shoulder facing out. Only his sharp corners are visible to me – his thigh, his elbow – should I be thrown off against him. When we get to school I barely hear his goodbye, but he closes the car door with unexpected consideration.

A few days ago we met outside the front door to the block, him carrying his backpack and me, heavy bags of shopping. He was ahead by a few steps, mumbled a hint of a greeting and left the door open for me before heading upstairs. But then, having dropped his burden on our landing, he came downstairs again to help, taking the potatoes and the mineral water pack hanging from my index finger, which was already turning blue. I thanked him, but there was no reply.

2

God helped my mother from the start, he came to her with the power of his voice to give meaning to her torment. He also gave her the courage to look for someone to print the funeral notices, the madness of having them posted in two or three spots in the accessible ring around the historic centre. Her daughter must not do without anything, in her death.

Some days I would drive past them and feel shame at seeing her plastered on the grey cement. One night I stopped, I tried the corner of a poster with a fingernail, but it was stuck fast, it didn't want to come off. I gave up almost at once. With my open hand I stroked the name, vowels and consonants. She had been my sister.

They fall apart ever so slowly, those posters. The shine from the glue goes first, then the ink starts to fade, and a little corner of the paper comes off at the top. Rain and wind work on that breach, insinuating themselves between wall and paper, until it starts to come off and folds onto itself, hiding the text. One morning they were gone.

My mother invokes him, her God, and is consoled. I, in my raw unbelief, imagine recognising him here on Earth and dragging him, by that blue mantle Sunday school children draw for him in their exercise books, through a guided tour of the disaster's ruins. She prays with measured fervour, for the dead one and the living. Our boy is quite gentle with his grandmother, he even looks at her, and lifts the corners of his mouth in an attempt to smile when she talks to him.

In the morning we leave together – he goes to school, I go to work, the other one tidies up then takes the bus to the cemetery. She takes a rather large bag containing all she deems necessary to tend to the graves, a cleaning product and a microfibre cloth. She buys flowers from the stall by the entrance, blowing half her pension on those. Every day is All Souls' Day for her. She performs the same meticulous gestures: throws away the old gerbera daisies, which are actually still fresh, and replaces them with new ones of a different colour, arranging them in the vase with soft fingers to show the bunch at its best. She polishes the white stone, the smile in the photo she chose herself. At almost regular intervals, she turns helplessly towards our neighbour, collapsed further down the row over the marble enclosing her own daughter.

The little girl was six on the night of the earthquake. My father is in another section – there was no space next to him. My mother neglects him a little, the recent bereavement has set him aside in her heart. She can tolerate a few days' dust on his portrait, the flower heads are allowed to droop and bend to gravity before they are replaced.

I go with her some Sundays. I stand aside while she works. At times I feel a sort of nausea and have to walk away. If the range and speed of her movements exceed a certain level, I feel seasick. I never say anything, taking a few steps back is enough. I leave her to her usual occupation, she needs it. Only at the beginning I protested weakly, about the posters, the photo on the headstone. She walks out of the gate as if satisfied, and stops a few minutes with the florist. They've become friends over time.

'I should get some pink gerberas tomorrow morning; shall I keep a bunch for you?'

'Yes, it's been a while since you had some, how come?'

'I don't know, who knows anything with these suppliers. But tomorrow, it's almost certain, I'll keep some for you.'

'In that case I'll take a few more, and replace my husband's flowers too, his are nearly wilted.'

'There's a discount if you buy two. Are you going shopping now? In this cold?'

Yes, she usually goes to the market on weekdays. Seasonal fruit and vegetables for us, those from the farmers, and then off home to make lunch. She takes the eleven-thirty bus; there are no more after that.

She has got used to the flat, she uses it for what it's for. At the start, the whiff of new was unbearable for her too. In the space of a month she managed to impregnate it with the delicate scents of healthy cooking. When we came, more than two years ago, we already knew we would find a bottle of bubbly in the fridge, from the government. The first thing I did was to open the bottle, without shaking it, rotating the cork slowly between my thumb and index finger to stop it popping. Then I drained it into the sink, holding it by the neck right down over the plug-hole. Once the pipe had guzzled it all, I dumped the bottle in the rubbish bin. My mother looked over respectfully, following me with her eyes.

Some of the older people from platforms four and five try to cultivate the unpaved ground around the C.A.S.E. They plant their seeds at the right time, get some allotments going. There are a few, one after the other, towards the road, precise rectangles. At harvest time, the old-age pensioners get downstairs more or less at the same time, they talk among their tomato plants, comment on the weather and show their neighbour from across the landing where parasites have attacked the skin of the fruit. I watch them on Sunday mornings, the cruellest day of the week, while smoking a cigarette at the window. They're so slow, standing among the vegetables in the light mist rising from the broken soil. On the stairs I spy the colours of the vegetables in their baskets, while they walk up to hand them to their wives. I'm surprised at their loyalty to the treacherous earth.

In autumn they methodically sweep up dead leaves, even when the wind spitefully blows them off right away to scratch the concreted square with their crumpled edges. They know the difference between useful and pointless actions, and alternate them in the constant effort to fill the time. When it snows they use light, wide-bladed shovels, the plastic ones you get now. They breathe out steam clouds as they work, the cold air stilling the tangle of wrinkles carved on faces reddened by cardiovascular disease.

My mother won't waste her green thumbs on this place – we'll leave anyway, she says, and she would be sorry to leave God's gift behind, that's what she calls it. So for us it's only geraniums on the balcony in summer, nothing more. We can take those with us. She dispenses daily water to them, tucks the soil back in or removes dried bits. They only give off their scent when touched.

She does not want to get used to this temporary accommodation. I see her measure out her contact with the neighbours so as not to get too close. But she does speak with reserved and compassionate consideration to the woman who has survived her little girl, when she occasionally lifts her head from the abyss.

The flat has three rooms: I gave mine to Marco when he came to stay with us two years ago, Mum and I share the other. She keeps it neat and clean, but displays the detachment of someone who waits with surreal patience to repair the house back in the village. It's a strange dream for someone no longer young; she says she owes it to dad, that his family had lived there for generations and he had refurbished the house himself, before getting married. I remind her warily that dad has been gone a long time, he doesn't know about the earthquake, and he won't know about a possible Reconstruction. What's that got to do with it? He sees everything from up there, she answers sternly, with the look she gave me when I told her I would not be confirmed. After a while she sits down, and as she half-closes her eyes she opens the old front door oiled by hand with a cloth. She steps into the vaguely musty smell of the tiny entrance hall and places her foot on the first step of the steep staircase leading up to where the voices of us twins echo shrilly, Olivia's happier and sharper. We were all alive, then.

3

I come across one of the squads patrolling the perimeter of
the Red Zone, and continue on for a few blocks among the
rare passers-by of the morning. After that, I don't need to
so much as push the barrier aside. I flatten myself against
the wall and slip into the shadow of the forbidden alley. I
walk uphill, already short of breath. From time to time a
stench of rotten wood reaches me in waves from supporting
beams still saturated with the night's rain. When I turn into
Via Mezzaluna I catch the movement of something dark
and furry in the corner of my eye, a small animal perhaps,
startled away. To get to my old studio I must walk past the
house that lost its façade, what's left inside now on display
– preserves and packs of pasta in the kitchen, the broken
bathroom mirror reflecting a cubist sky, clothes clinging to
their hangers in the open wardrobe, sleeves helplessly fading
in the sun. A light switch that has lost its wall hangs by its
cable and swings in the emptiness. Nausea rises within me, I
control it. It's that gentle swinging; I just need to look away,
walk further.

I used to work on the ground floor of a building now
classified category E unusable. I unlock the frozen padlock
binding together the two halves of the front door, but then I
have to force the seemingly looser half with my hands, and
that's not enough. I put my shoulder into it, my knee, until
I overcome the friction of walnut wood against the floor.
The screeching noise is overwhelming in the vast silence.
Instinctively I reach out to press the button on the right, the

light won't come on. I take a few cautious steps as I adjust to the half-light. My shoes raise a din of broken crockery, and dust, which I breathe in. I find the only window by memory, and this time the shutters respond meekly.

I have never been back, since the earthquake. When I decided to resume work elsewhere, I sent someone to load the kiln and little else, just the essentials. I stocked up on ready-to-paint pieces from a craft workshop in Castelli, and new brushes, pigments and glazes, even a few lustres. From the market in Piazza d'Armi I got a large plastic tub to prepare the glaze and a long wooden spoon for mixing.

Only the finished pieces are safe, packed in large boxes stacked against the back wall. I could take them with me and sell them. Everything else has fallen from the shelves that span the width of the walls, sliding along planes tilted by the earthquake. The discontinuous lines drawn by the broken pieces outline a precise, if reduced, floor map of the large room. On one side, a rubble of crumbled bisque pottery; further on, the glazed bottles set down to dry and at the other end, ready for the kiln, the plates with the cockerel and the apothecary jars with the sixteenth-century motif. All that I had made is lost.

I pick up a fragment and read my thin signature, interrupted at the 'E', under a berry. Then, like a small miracle, I find a little bell, thrown intact into one of my rubber clogs. I blow on it and turn it slowly, closely following the flower design along its border. It was meant for Easter 2009. I check that it rings, with that minuscule clapper. The gentle sound acts as an alarm, I'm wasting time, this isn't what I came for. I slip it into my bag and look for the drawings.

The folders are in the middle of the table, next to the jars and the reject tiles used for colour tests. One of these has moved and is now balanced on the edge, half on and half off. I return it to safety with the others and it leaves a clean trail between dust and dust. On sheets of paper warped by humidity, the drawings are in good condition. I will be able to use them again. Only here and there the ink has dribbled a little. I'm about to go out, files under my arm, but then give in to the temptation to salvage the old dungarees with multi-coloured stains that I used to wear in here. I take them off the hook, burdened by grains of exploded plaster.

Outside the day air is so clear it hurts. The wind blows from the nearest face of Mount Sirente, squeezing through the narrow lanes aligned with it like fingers into a glove. It brings the smell of snow, of resins thickening on tree trunks. I have to shield my eyes to look at the house across the lane, wrapped round in blue containment bands. On the first floor, a dirty white curtain slides lazily out of the open doorway onto the balcony, dances a little and retreats, then again, obeying the whims of the air that moves it. From there once wafted the scents of Signora Leda's fragrant herbal teas, in the afternoons. She was nice, suffered from arthritis, a bit of a gossip. If her legs let her, she would get down the stairs and across with a full cup trembling in its saucer, if not, she'd call from the window to invite me up. I would climb the steps to the warm and steamy kitchen. She liked to list the names of the blends she used, always different: blazing hearth, winter garden, enchanted wood. When I didn't feel inclined to listen to her I would make the excuse that I was at a delicate stage of the work, and wouldn't go. I painted her a teapot with fruits and flowers from her infusions, the initials 'LB' over the blueberries. It must've broken too.

I hardly ever think of Leda.

But now I pull the weeds grown tall and undisturbed outside her front door, in the spaces between the cobbles. They have already seeded, the winter has turned them dry and fierce. They resist and cut into my palm. Busy as I am uprooting them, I hear too late the engine approaching the end of the lane, down Via Cascina. I don't have time to hide, I cover my ears and wait. It's only an instant; the armoured military vehicle passes quickly by and the two soldiers in camouflage uniform don't look my way. I see them in the cab, chatting and laughing.

What's left vibrates and shudders, then the noise softens in the distance and a deathly quiet returns, spreading out over the neighbourhood. I find my way back to the car park down a long and convoluted route, keeping well away from Via del Drago. I choose a safe passage out of the Red Zone – the patrols hardly ever pass it, I've heard. The window of my stationary car reflects my shoulders, dirty from all the walls I have skirted along the way.

4

In the beginning we were two murky clumps of cells, still presumed to be one by our parents. We grew, immersed in the sweet ocean that was our mother, as it slowly reduced around us. One day in those nine months, with the smooth, expansive movement of a small body turning in his sleep, the foetus Olivia moved to the front, right under the stretched surface of the belly. There, a suspicion of light and the indistinct, muffled sound of the world seeped through. There, it was still possible to expand, increasing the radius of the incomplete sphere along with the tension of our mother's skin. Olivia did that. I got stuck behind, in my sac, between her and the hard rings of the adult spine. I did my time in this tight space, in the dark, in silence. My sister intercepted external waves and influences, and kept them to herself. The circular caresses of the open hand were all for her, all her prominence exposed to the world. My only nourishment came from the umbilical cord, from the blood.

So I imagined our intrauterine lives, when I was around eight. I was certain I had suffered a supreme disadvantage which justified all my weaknesses. I used to want to listen again and again to the tale of our birth, Olivia's extra grams and centimetres, her thick helmet of hair and the additional feeds she claimed with unbearable wails. My modest hunger satisfied, I would go back to the cot and she was again attached to the breast for that portion of additional milk I believed to have been thicker, more concentrated, a deeper yellow, even. As children we wore identical clothes in different sizes, mine always one smaller. They often called us Olivia and her twin or, even worse, Olivia and the other one.

'Yours is a queen's name and it intimidates a little, that's why they won't say it,' our mother consoled me when I asked her why.

In our last year at primary school, I noticed a bad boy from the village point me to his gang as I walked by. He would whisper something and they'd all start to laugh. They were in secondary school already. My sister observed them in surly silence. One afternoon we were strolling down from the church youth club and the boy was sitting on a stone fence on our way, already observing us from a distance. Olivia was walking a few steps ahead in the unseasonal June stuffiness. He didn't say anything to her but when I walked past his dangling legs, he sung to himself three times 'here comes the rough draft,' stretching his foot to touch me. She came back and looked him up and down before yanking him by the hem of his trousers, and threw him to the ground. Terrified, my head in my hands, I admired her for hitting like a boy, with no scratching or hair-pulling. She was pounding him with her fists, taking only a few punches in return, advantaged by his surprise. She finally got up and left him dribbling in the dust, delivering one last kick to his backside. Then she recovered the dishevelled catechism books from the cobbles, hers and mine. I wasn't aware I'd dropped them. As we started on our way home she brushed my cheek, a caress soiled by a bully. It was her apology for the violence used in my defence, the promise to protect me for life, even from her own superiority.

Later our mother went through the motions of telling her off a little. She said that some things should be reported to her or Dad, not settled with fisticuffs.

'It's not as if you're nobody's children,' she concluded. She was cleaning her up with non-stinging disinfectant and a gentle touch, ensuring from time to time that I was still there behind her, ready with the clean dressings. As always, she was more worried about me than about Olivia, and the bruises blooming on her face.

The following day we were meant to have our school photos taken, in groups but also for individual pupils who might want them. The photographer hesitated an instant when Olivia casually sat at a desk, with 'HURRAH FOR YEAR 5B' chalked on the blackboard just behind her.

'Do you want one by yourself too?' he asked with a nod at the landscape of bruises.

'One by myself and one with my sister,' she replied, adjusting her hair. Before posing with a pen in her hand pretending to write, she pulled out of her pocket a pair of dark glasses she'd got from who knows where and wore them over her black eye and bruised smile. In the lens, a ten-year old diva, heroic and smug.

Looking back, the punch-up turned out to be the faithful mirror of the uneven relationship between us twins. We never escaped its frame, bewitched by the fear of losing each other. And the battle-face portrait from that last year at primary school has over the years risen in position in my internal album, gaining importance over other images that have marked instants of our lives.

Later, when our features became more defined, insignificant details made her bright and charming, and me more ordinary. The difference of a few millimetres' distance between the eyes, a slightly warmer skin tone, the mouth with a more marked cupid's bow. I see this every day when I paint, a little is enough to make a difference.

At secondary school we were in different classes but not far away from each other. Halfway through the morning I'd feel her presence cross the wall and unfurl through my classroom, invisible to the others. Just as now, while I work, her absence unfurls. I decide to pause; the energy is draining from my hands in any case, towards my wrists, my arms, my heart. I walk to the large window overlooking the countryside. In passing I stroke the round mahogany table I used to have in my sitting room. Olivia and I found it at an antiques fair, a nineteenth-century English piece. A real bargain, the seller had sworn. I've cleaned the earthquake off it and brought it here, for now, to stand on its brass wheels. I don't know if sooner or later I will rebuild a home around this wood so pleasant to the touch, the marks of those who owned it before now wiped clean.

There's always a lot of light outside, even on these short winter days. Often I manage to paint in the sunlight that filters through the glass, without having to turn on any lights. And I'm never cold, the old cast-iron burner heats the room well – the landlord was right. In exchange for a little rent he has given me the use of the villa's ground floor, tons of firewood and a large table pushed against the external wall for working in the open air in the good season. This place must be a family inheritance, but I don't know anything about it: I'll ask the postwoman. The landlord lives in Bologna and comes back once a month, at the weekend, and stops over for two weeks at Christmas and all of August. To myself, I refer to him as 'the professor'; I know he teaches at the university. On his last visit before the holidays he bought a large box of my objects for gifts. He seems sincere, or perhaps he just wants to help.

Olivia would like it here. It's strange we missed the place on our interminable drives. She would now be sitting with her back to the window, intently watching me work. When I think about it the paint goes mad. It clots and refuses to flow, shrinking into itself, or instead becomes too liquid and drips over the dried glaze. The brush catches on the microscopic bumps of the baked surface.

I'm cast away on an island where nothing happened; there are no fault lines near here, and the villa had been remodelled some time ago. But the ruins of a hamlet razed by the whim of the earthquake are on display on the hill up ahead, and in the opposite direction, all the way down, that indistinct blotch is L'Aquila. Seen from here it could still be the legendary city of the ninety-nine churches and ninety-nine fountains. I could arrange to meet someone tonight at the Bright Fountain and go for a late beer in the town centre, after a film at the Rex. At seven in the morning the bells of San Pietro would wake me up and I'd walk to work taking my usual shortcuts through the lanes.

5

Marco came one afternoon, in the pouring rain.

We met him at the car park under our platform, among the anti-seismic insulators. He accepted our four kisses on the cheeks and unloaded his bags on the concrete floor, then walked away a few steps. Roberto, my sister's estranged husband, came slowly out of the car, like an old man, and after greeting us with his eyes down he started right away on the issue of the maintenance cheque, as if it could be transferred from his dead wife to us. I renewed our refusal, made several times already over the phone. You can put it in the bank for your son, my mother conceded, cold as ice. I spoke briefly of Marco's new school, of the books we had easily procured. Thankfully it was still only October, the one after the earthquake.

The boy didn't pay attention to our stilted conversation, he'd immediately put on his headphones, connected to who knows what. We could hear scraps of escaping music cackle faintly in the silence already fallen among us adults. He paced up and down kicking an imaginary football; occasionally his unlaced shoes would hiss as they brushed against the cement.

He had lasted in Rome with his father a little over six months, what was left of the spring after the earthquake and the uneventful summer, barricaded in an impenetrable muteness. His grandmother and I had seen him and heard from him several times in the first period of our mourning, but he hadn't been any more talkative with us. Instead, my brother-in-law had often called to moan about Marco's exploits. When he wanted to make us feel sorry for him, and wasn't able to, he'd say 'your nephew'. My nephew had slashed his new partner's car tyres, that same young violinist he had left Olivia for.

'She's been so considerate,' Roberto declaimed without shame. 'She moved to another neighbourhood before Marco arrived, to leave us to ourselves.' Painfully awkward pauses in the conversation took the place of my expected responses.

'She comes from time to time and cooks us something special, but the boy won't even sit at the table ...' he'd start whining again. Marco would rather eat crackers, or fresh air. During one of those visits he'd gone downstairs and ripped her car tyres open.

'With a kitchen knife, imagine that,' marvelled Roberto.

And there I betrayed my sympathy for the young saboteur: 'What else was he supposed to use? A scalpel?'

When my occasional remarks disappointed his expectations, the tale would be enriched with ever more striking episodes, in the attempt to elicit a minimum of indignation.

'He must've read our messages ... He sent her obscene texts from my mobile, that's what we've got to. He's even barefaced denied the evidence, he says it wasn't him. Actually, he doesn't say anything, he just shakes his head.'

Marco persevered in his uncompromising refusal to speak to his only parent. In the meantime, he had been moved from second to third year of secondary school, in consideration of the trauma he'd suffered.

When his grandmother and I had last heard from him, he'd seemed interested in the news of our transfer to one of the flats in the C.A.S.E. Project, at Coppito Three. That same evening, out of the blue, he had addressed his father, only to communicate that he would come and live with us, if we could accommodate him. Roberto took a few days to come round to this being the best solution. He would repeat that incessantly in the frequent phone calls of that week. For him and for everyone, for him and for everyone, he'd mumble feverishly, without finding the guts to say 'for me', which would've been an inconvenient truth.

While we were still there, in the car park, a wind picked up, slanting the rain to hit the car bonnets in the outer row. A man from the first floor arrived in his economy car, leaving wet trails over several metres. It was starting to get cold under the platform and we'd been standing in silence for around two minutes, the time multiplied by our deep discomfort. All three of us were concentrating our gaze on Marco, dressed far too lightly for such a harsh climate. Roberto clawed at that detail in his last attempt to reach his son before leaving him.

'Why don't you put a jumper on?' he asked in a loud but already resigned voice, and the other stood for an instant, fixing him sideways, his closed mouth twisted in a grimace of mild disgust. He then moved his bags a few metres further away from the car that had brought him, as if to facilitate an overdue departure, and went back to walking around in the damp, thick air in his Nirvana T-shirt.

I hugged myself, trembling. Roberto understood then.

'It's getting late, I have a concert in Rome tonight,' he whispered. He seemed very weak. There was no reason to invite him in.

To avoid saying goodbye to his father, Marco showed a sudden interest in a dog that was wandering about looking for the right car to pee against. My mother and I watched him leave, the hunched musician inside his empty vehicle. The boy came closer once the car had disappeared towards the trunk road. Then we went up in single file carrying the bags, him stomping on the steps. I opened the door for him and he went in hardly breathing; after a handful of seconds he even turned red. I instinctively headed to the balcony and he, grasping for a way out, took it. But the rain dripped implacable from the balcony above, through the gaps between the planks, that's how they'd made them. He stayed there for a little while, breathing and getting wet. Water dripped from the tip of his nose and the ends of his curls were pulled and stretched by the weight of the rain. His grandmother couldn't resist for long and rescued him with a towel.

'Come in and change,' she begged him. 'You'll catch your death.'

While I was preparing hot chocolate on the stove, my mother put a warm apple cake on the table. Once cut, it gave off a scent of still-soft butter, cinnamon and lemon, grains of sugar forming on the surface. Marco nibbled half a slice and took a few hot and noisy sips. The chocolate drew on him the same Dali moustaches as the thousands of capfuls of milk and chocolate he had consumed as a child. He remained sitting in his desolation, abandoned to our impotent care.

Later I ushered him into the spruced-up bedroom, the curtains in shades of orange and yellow and the bedspread to match. He threw himself on the bed and instantly fell asleep, as if he had fainted. At dinnertime his grandmother was tormented by the question of waking him or not. I managed to persuade her of the limited danger of one missed meal, took his stinking shoes off and covered him for the night.

In the morning, a new bloom of spots had flowered on his apathetic face.

6

In winter, the darkest and coldest hour before dawn is when they come to collect the rubbish from the C.A.S.E. I have been awake for some time; my mother's breathing in the other bed has become imperceptible to my accustomed ears. In the flat next door, or perhaps the one above, a chest is wracked by a persistent cough, obstinate and unnerving. It falls quiet for a short spell, then starts again. From an indefinable distance a dog barks again and again, always the same dog. Three deep throat notes, repeated every few seconds, awaken a sort of visceral anxiety, restarting the motion of faeces in my bowels. The wind has the same effect as it blows on the windowpanes, almost pushing them into the darkened rooms.

As night nears its end, I wait for the rubbish collectors. I recognise them as they turn off the trunk road, from the noise of the gears going down. I imagine two men behind truck windows misted by their breath: I follow them as they approach the rubbish bins and get off the truck to empty them, a few steps on the tarmac and they go back inside, the doors closing one after the other. The driver grabs the wheel, his hands in protective gloves, and engages the whining reverse. First, second, and they're off, the engine melting into a still unbroken darkness. They leave, unaware of the intimacy that has briefly linked us. At every stop, the affront of the cold reminds them they're alive.

Sometimes I can hear Marco sleeping in the next room, as he turns and speaks unknown languages in tones deeper than his daytime voice. If I can muster my strength, I go in and tuck in the blankets scattered by his dreams. While he lies unaware, I caress his hair and the forehead furrowed by mysterious adventures. He was moaning this morning around five – even his grandmother heard him.

Stay in bed, I whispered to her, and got up without turning on the light. In the passageway between the two rooms I stumbled on something soft and fell headlong on the floor, banging my head against the door jamb. I figured out what had happened before I picked myself up, by the stench of Marco's shoes. I tell him every day not to leave them lying around. I kicked them out of the way with my slippered feet, much to my mother's disapproval. He kept on sleeping like a baby, he'd even stopped moaning.

My right middle finger, bent by the fall, was only a little sore at first and I went back under the covers, to warm myself up if anything. By seven I'd decided to take my finger, now a throbbing sausage, to A&E, where I was logged in as a non-emergency white code. The nurse smiled at the visible bump on my forehead, that I'd forgotten all about.

After waiting hours for a no-fractures diagnosis, they start to get busy with bandages and splints. I beg the technician to leave my thumb and index finger free, if possible.

'What do you need them for?' he wants to know while he immobilises them at the base. I vaguely mention urgent deliveries, ceramics to paint.

'Ah, my mother adores ceramics, but anyway this finger, how did you ...?' He questions me with renewed curiosity.

'I tripped on my nephew's shoes, in the dark,' I respond calmly and he laughs, shaking his head. 'You won't be able to paint,' he adds, mercilessly.

I walk out of the glass door and there he is, the cheek of him, sitting at the end of the waiting room with all that hair, the overlong limbs he doesn't know what to do with, folded like a collapsible ruler, backpack slung under the blue plastic chair. With his eyes covered by the electrified fringe, he either pretends not to have, or really hasn't, seen me. I walk right past him and keep going; he's even wearing the very same shoes. I walk along the corridor and turn towards the exit. Suddenly I am assailed by the doubt that he may not be there for me. Perhaps he isn't feeling well, after all he should be at school by now. I run back, turn the corner and we bump into each other. I nearly take his eye out with the contraption on my middle finger. A choked cry escapes him.

I set upon him right away with a flurry of questions, keeping my face hard.

'What are you doing here instead of being at school? Who brought you? Why on earth can't you be more careful with your stuff? Have you seen this mess?'

People walk past and look at us, they are sure to believe us mother and son. I wait for the counterattack and instead he turns almost completely away, in silence. I know that's what he does to hide his tears. I look at my splintered finger and wish I could amputate it out of shame, together with my tongue, and take both like cut flowers to wilt on my sister's grave. I try to call his name softly, my voice cracks. I touch his arm and he doesn't pull away, his elbow does not collide with my stomach as I deserve. I apologise; I tell him I'd been asking for it, my accursed habit of walking around in the dark, nothing's broken anyway, only a slight sprain, he mustn't worry. I tighten my hand a little and feel how fragile and hard he is under the down padding.

We remain still for another few minutes, then move in silent agreement.

'How will you manage to drive?' he asks. I hadn't thought about that. 'I'll help you hold the wheel,' he offers, 'so you can change gears with your left hand.'

He's good – it must be all the video games. We choose a longer route, and as the kilometres roll by I loosen my grip and leave the steering almost entirely to him. He laughs abruptly and slaps his knee.

'Your middle finger will get stuck like that,' he observes. 'It'll show even more because of the splint.' One after the other, he answers all my earlier questions.

'We had a student meeting the last few hours. Granny signed me a note so I could leave early and I came to see how you were, on the number seven. In A&E that nurse, the one with the moustache, she said they hadn't fixed you up yet. I've been in touch with Granny in the meantime, she was a bit worried about you this morning.'

An unusual cheerfulness comes over us as we drive. I might even feel a little hungry. Marco suddenly swerves to avoid a car indicating right and turning left instead. He articulates unrepeatable abuse, already an expert motorist. Then, as we get closer to Coppito Three, our giggles become strained, almost jarring, our voices distorted like my finger, ringing false in the attempt to maintain a spirit we no longer feel. We're trying to hold on to a moment of grace, take a little home perhaps, to share with Granny. By the time Marco engages the handbrake it's all over, we've come back to ourselves.

Upstairs I bring my mother up to date. Lunch is ready. Through the columns of thin vapour snaking upward from our respective plates, I read in his eyes my same concern for what seems like a mountain of homemade *tagliatelle*. They appear thicker and darker than usual, their surface even coarser.

'Are they spelt?' I guess. Yes, they are. Strange, we never use this type of flour. Steel scrapes porcelain when I try to roll with my left hand a forkful of what was once one of my favourite dishes. Nobody here ever really feels any desire for food, starting with my mother. She eats to show us a good example.

7

On the coach to Rome, I listen absent-mindedly to the girl next to me talking to her boyfriend on the phone. She steers the conversation like a skilful female, hanging up at the right time; he calls back and she ups the ante. I rest my temple on the cold glass that the rain is painting with thin oblique drops in the dark. We breeze over the viaducts; we'll be there in less than an hour. All I have with me is a spacious shoulder bag. I slip my left hand inside and reassure myself with the touch of the little box of pills and the full bottle in a carrier bag. This time I have booked a different hotel from the one of previous years; according to the website it has various levels and hundreds of rooms. I will hang the 'do not disturb' sign on the door and nobody will notice that I never leave the room. I can't do that near home – a middle-aged woman would come gently knocking in the soft light of the corridor, asking, are you well, can I get you anything.

I told my mother I'm going to see a friend in Rome and will be back the day after tomorrow, in time for lunch. She will have noticed the coincidence with the date, and my same escape on the previous two occasions. No problem, off you go, she said, but she came with me to the landing and watched me going down the stairs as one watches someone setting off on a long journey, uncertain of their return. I asked her to say goodbye to Marco for me and forced myself into a sort of smile, before disappearing from view.

The girl next to me communicates to the same interlocutor that we will arrive at nineteen fifteen, not at a quarter past seven. Mind you, he'd better be on time to help her with the suitcase, too heavy for her. Be sure you're there, it's only twenty minutes away. It's true, the coach's luminous display says the same.

Tomorrow is our birthday. The third, since. I couldn't have stayed at home, I would have been useless. Tomorrow I would have nothing for the son who has lost a mother, the mother who has lost a daughter, I could not console them. My very presence would confirm that it's the best one who is missing.

On this day, by this time, we would have taken all but two shelves out of the fridge, to make space for the identical cakes that occupied it, one at the bottom, one at the top. For the filling, my mother would have got hold of fresh cow's milk and free-range eggs from the women who came to sell their own produce in the market square. An old widowed aunt would store the everyday food that had been evicted, and we'd take her a generous portion of cake in return. I don't know if she really was our aunt or if we just called her that, as it's done. Olivia always waited for the moment she'd be left alone with me and the fridge to swipe a fingerful of coffee cream off the side of the sponge cake, where it would be less noticeable. With a nod she'd invite me to do the same, and if I was scared of getting caught she'd shove her own tasty finger in my mouth. Then, still with her hands, she would level the pale surface like a builder smoothing out a fault in the plaster. Just to make sure, she'd gently turn the cake around so the meddled-with side would be at the back and therefore not visible, not yet at least.

We did that many times. Even when we were both living in L'Aquila, each on her own, we'd try to go back to the village at least one day early, to sleep together the night before. Dad would have made sure the Muscat wine was cold in good time, we'd take it to our big-girls room and the cork

37

would pop at midnight on the dot, the time our celebrations started. After a first toast on our feet, the bottle would be passed from one bed to the other, dripping on the bedside cabinet. Between the laughter and the bubbles, it became a choking hazard – we never drank like that.

The tradition was broken with Marco's birth: Olivia would no longer come. I might go over to hers for birthday wishes, but the attention of both was all for that curly-haired baby boy. Later, when they moved to Rome because Roberto was now playing with a new quintet, all that was left of our celebrations was a phone call. We'd have to wait until they came back, on a weekend, and then we'd all get together for a family meal, a much richer one than usual as if to make up for the creeping feeling of a missed anniversary. The two cakes had become one, a gentle indication that our parents, now grandparents, had finally accepted the passage of their daughters into adulthood.

The man at reception checks me in without even looking at me and I am glad I needn't look at him. I go up to my room.

The night passes, somehow. The heavy curtains smell of dust and stale smoke when I pull them as far as they will go against the rising sun, painful blade to my dilated pupils. I sit on the unmade bed, facing the bedside table. In the narrow light of the lamp I pour a cognac from the bottle I took with me, the ten Tavor pills lined up on the wood veneer surface. I taste the bitterness of the first one on my tongue, a sip of spirit scorches membranes that had gone so long without it. I swallow another pill, a sip of cognac and another, another, another, always chased by a sip that never empties the immensely capacious glass. Or perhaps I have refilled it once or twice. I feel the entire length of my oesophagus burning, the protest of my empty stomach. I resist. I repress the impulse to vomit with an emotionless swallowing sequence. I flick the switch and wrap myself in blankets. A twin once more, I sleep my temporary death in this large dark womb.

I wake at an undetermined time of the evening. I throw up, I don't know where. After that, I fall into a second stretch of hours, shorter this time. Finally I turn on the bedside lamp and vomit a little more chloridric acid on the floor, between the bed and the rug. My head is a crazed and throbbing beehive; slowly it begins to reacquaint itself with its body, with the weakness of it. I drink water from the tap in the bathroom basin. I carefully avoid the mirror and spend a long time in the shower, mindful of the bandages on my injured hand. Then I dry the alien and unfeeling skin, a desert of cells the blood takes time to flow to, the nerves struggling to reactivate. During the sleeping day the organism has been reduced to a beating inner clump, a little nucleus of condensed life, and from there restarts a wave of stored heat, towards the dull, pale skin. The tissues prepare to receive nourishment, the cycle starts again. I do not object.

I open the curtains. The time I wanted to lose is already yesterday. On another yesterday further back in time, I helped my mother to wash her, dress her. At first there was someone else with us in that vast, freezing room, an indistinct figure in the background, against the white wall. A woman, I'm sure, I don't know who. She must have left later, left us to ourselves when she realised we had found the strength, there and then, to do what was needed. We would not have let anyone take care of Olivia's nude body, her defenceless orifices, her squashed chest. She hindered us passively, with a mineral rigidity. A coarse dust covered her, the hands and unblemished face in particular, like a heavy face powder for an unspeakable carnival parade. We couldn't wash her hair, we were only able to shake it free of the dry, crumbly dirt. She was beautiful in the end. We looked at her and kissed her, a kiss on her forehead from me, and many, many kisses from her mother, on her feet, hands, cheeks and head, caressing her. Only then did she bathe her in tears, not before, while she was working. She spoke to her for a long time, words I don't remember.

Olivia was ready to meet Marco. I don't remember anything of that either, or perhaps I walked away.

At the last minute I cut a lock of hair, from the nape of her neck or she never would have forgiven me, and took her with me. I keep her in a little box covered with flower-printed paper. From time to time I open it to see if at least this lock can remain the same in the time that separates it from her. For now, the only perceptible change is that the hairs look a little dry, opaque – you immediately feel the difference when you touch them between thumb and index finger. They are not attached to life.

I go out in the metallic light of the early morning. I dispose of the remaining alcohol in the rubbish bin, nod at the barista who after an appraising look suggests a strong coffee. He serves it to me in one of those thick-walled cups I used to have at home; the earthquake has broken almost all of them. He serves three small pastries alongside the coffee, and I eat them dutifully. I pay and wave at him on the way out, realising I haven't pronounced a single syllable. I walk towards Tiburtina station.

I am hindered by a stall being set up on the pavement, old comic books in cardboard boxes. The man has opened a box of *Dylan Dog* issues and arranges them at the front. On impulse I phone Marco, he'll be having his breakfast milk by now. When I question him, he lists the back issues he's missing, surprised. And yes, Granny's fine; we hang up quickly, he's already a little late. I find three, what luck, and they weigh less than the cognac in my bag. I must hurry now – my legs are up to the challenge.

The return coach is half-empty. I take a window seat quite far back, but my place doesn't save me from an acquaintance who comes up and decides to sit next to me. She starts chatting, asks about the immobilised finger and tells me when she came to the capital, to do what and how. After a short pause she expects me to do the same. I don't respond right away. I look out at the countryside around Rome running away in the window, then I excuse myself: I have to move a little to the front, the usual motion sickness. Of course, no problem. She doesn't have the courage to follow me.

The driver slows down to take the L'Aquila west exit. A thin mist lingers by the toll booth, something out of a barren season. The town offers no panoramas to those returning, it takes us in, that's all, crumples my throat with this welcome of criss-crossing cracks on façades, intermediate storeys reduced in number, pillars twisted on their axis. I voluntarily return to the place that killed my sister.

8

Marco comes in, ungainly, throws his backpack behind the door and goes to the bathroom, scraping one jean-clad leg against the other. He went to a friend's house for lunch and stayed on to study, he'd told his grandmother. Once back in the living room, he bumps his elbow into the bag I left on a piece of furniture, and knocks it to the floor. He picks it up and puts it back where it was, holding it as it if were a worm. Every time his legs, feet or any edge of his body stray from the imaginary bubble I keep him in, he gets into trouble. He's not used to his own height, reached in such a short time, not yet aware of how to gauge his movements to avoid collisions with the world. I hand him the comic books I bought in Rome. He grabs them nervously and puts them down somewhere, without even looking at them. Strange – when I asked him about the missing back issues on the phone this morning he'd seemed happy. But what can I expect, after yesterday. I left him again, on this birthday.

There he is, at the table in front of me as usual. My mother had her dinner early and went out to attend a memorial Mass for the victims of the earthquake. She doesn't even try asking us to go with her. Here I am, sitting in front of him, his averted eyes, his head bent over the colourful plate. He tosses his voice at me across his distance.

'Why did the earthquake destroy some parts of the town and left others almost intact?'

'What do you mean?' I take my time, frightened by the direct question. He has never mentioned this before.

'I mean, in Via XX Settembre buildings collapsed and all those students died. Other people too, Mum's dentist. In Via Strinella, which follows right on, there was only a bit of damage. My school friend Rash lives there.'

'It depends on how the buildings were erected, on the materials. They used poor-quality cement, there were not enough reinforcement bars in it, and they were thin and smooth. The people responsible can't even be taken to court, they've managed to die of old age. And the geologists have analysed the soil too. In Via XX Settembre they'd built on reclaimed land, the least suitable,' I explain, wiping my suddenly clammy hands on a napkin.

'What does that mean?'

'That the soil had been excavated and transported there from the foundations of buildings in neighbouring areas. Like that would be enough to support a five- or six-storey building in an earthquake.'

'What about the old town centre?' he presses on.

'Many houses just didn't make it. Previous restorations weren't earthquake-proof,' I continue, looking at the leftover meat going cold and hard on my plate.

'Why did mine collapse?' His voice is raised, a few drops of saliva sting my face.

'I don't know. Your mother and I trusted an expert; he came to inspect our houses after the first tremors, mine and yours both. Granny's house too, in the village. He promised us we'd be safe.' I shuffle uneasily in my chair.

'Who is that bastard?' he shouts and his voice, not quite adult yet, slips into a farcical falsetto.

'Calm down. It doesn't matter any more. I wouldn't even know where to look for him.' My answer stumbles under his spitting rage.

'Ah, it doesn't, does it?! They'd checked Rash's house too and said there was no danger, but that building didn't come down! Perhaps his parents didn't ask the same genius you relied on,' he wheezes accusingly.

'Why do you take it out on us? Where could we have found someone to predict that earthquake? Marco, the experts on the Risk Committee had reassured everyone and that's why they've been found guilty now. None of us could possibly think ...' I spread my arms, defeated.

'Of course not! And even now, nobody knows anything. All these shitheads going on about reclaimed land, nobody knows why one building collapsed and another didn't!' He fidgets under the table and our feet clash; his lower lip, dry and drained of blood, is stirred by a fine tremor. My blunted intuition is enough to understand that that he is jealous of his friend Fabio, known as Rash, not for his habitable flat but for his still living mother.

He has barricaded himself behind his hair, but shortly after he looks up from the salad he's been fiddling with for ten minutes and abruptly announces, 'You have to come to school tomorrow.'

The class coordinator invites me to follow her into the multimedia classroom. I walk to the rhythm of her heels, in the wake of overpowering perfume. She shows me two computers that have been tampered with by Marco. They look fine but they won't switch on – he has messed them up. A technician has already inspected them, the damage cannot be fixed. They were almost new, donated by I don't quite hear who, after 6th April, three years ago. She goes on to explain in detail how serious this is for the school, given the chronic lack of funds.

'Are you sure my nephew is responsible for this?' I ask and she, ready, pulls out a telephone from her bag and runs footage of the vandalism under my nose. It was filmed by a boy in the same class who, when grilled by the headmaster along with the rest, handed it in. Coward, I think too loudly. The teacher hears me and fixes me with a severe stare.

We are now sitting on opposite sides of a desk. She's holding onto the edge with pincer-like hands, her thumbs underneath the surface. I concentrate on her fingers, soft from moisturiser applied this morning, on her various rings, the nails lacquered with a light varnish, almost a flesh colour, the total absence of cuticles. She has never had to dig in the rubble, I imagine. She talks of the boy, his head always in the clouds, shame, so clever, they never would have thought him capable of this. Then she changes her tone and pushes her impeccable hairdo towards me; she becomes maternal, conspiratorial. 'I understand your situation,' she says.

'What situation do you understand?' I ask, and she flounders, unbalanced for an instant before composing herself again into her role.

'The family situation, madam,' she murmurs, as if there were people inside the fireproof cabinet, trying to listen in. 'It's only for this reason that we have decided to suspend Marco from class instead of excluding him.'

She seems almost pleased, as I view through her eyes a panorama of foreign, distant suffering.

'There is no need for you to try and understand,' I rebut, already on my feet. 'Just send me the bill for the damage.'

'Anyway, there was no need for you to come.' It's her final shot. 'We have called in his father.'

'I came because Marco asked me to,' I clarify.

One last question: I want to know precisely when this happened. The day before yesterday, as I expected, the day I have refused to acknowledge for the past three years. While I slept my chemical sleep elsewhere, here Marco was trying to get by as well as he could.

I shake the right hand extended by the teacher with my left, with no enthusiasm. This time I go before her. I hear her heels clicking behind me, and spare myself the perfume. I wait for Marco outside the M.U.S.P. in the sickly sunlight, nearly the end of the school day. He spots me right away and comes closer. He searches my eyes, finds them hard; I had nearly forgotten the colour of his. He offers me a feeble *ciao*, trembling, almost. A few steps behind his classmates look on, worried.

'Let's go, the car is over there.' I point sourly. Inside the car he angles himself towards me by a few degrees. I manage to drive by myself. I recognise the laboured breathing that prepares for speech without producing any. To feel him suffer like this is unbearable. I slow down and ask, 'What's going on, Marco?'

'Will you tell my father? Will you tell Granny?' he barely whispers.

'I won't tell Granny. I won't tell your father either – I hardly ever speak to him. But I know the school has called him.'

He sighs, shifts in his seat and we're home. I turn the engine off; he touches my arm and a murmur escapes him. 'Nothing like this will ever happen again.' But then, suddenly: 'Actually, get him to pay for it,' and he gets out, slamming the door.

He sees before I do the neighbour who lost her little girl in the earthquake. She is so weightless and weak that she can't press the pedal that opens the wheelie bin. Marco does it for her – he even takes the bag and slings it inside.

9

It must be a month since the last time. Now he calls, after what Marco got up to in school. The appointment is at the newly reopened Piazza Duomo. We walk along the perimeter, through patches of shade, and he talks. At the first question, how are things, I pretend not to hear. At his second, about my mother, I shrug my shoulders. He tells me about his difficulties with his son, often he won't even bother to answer the phone, he never calls back. On the day of Olivia's birthday, he says, he tried again and again without getting through. I can't bear him speaking her name so lightly, I really can't stand it.

'Was it so important, what you wanted to say to him?' I bark.

'Well, you know, it's a painful anniversary for all of you. I wanted to hear him,' he justifies, appeasingly.

'You can bet it was painful for us. And you, the widower, did you have a good day? Or are you not the widower? Can you become a widower if you were separated?' I insist.

'Leave it,' he mutters. We walk silently for a while after that, avoiding the confrontation. Then he starts again about Marco, he can never get him to go to Rome, and when he comes over himself for the afternoon, his son escapes him with all sorts of excuses. Today, for example, they won't meet. He sent him a message a little while ago, but he says he has too much work on, imagine!

'He won't forgive me for not being there the night of the earthquake,' he continues in a low voice. I turn to look at him for an instant, impressed by his insight. To be more precise, Marco won't forgive him for leaving them, and the consequences of that.

I find him thinner, a little shabby, bleary-eyed. He's wearing a blue jumper under his open jacket. He must have washed it himself, a greasy stain endures in the middle of his chest. He has aged prematurely, the lines on his face are few but deep as wounds, the wrinkles at the sides of his mouth concealed by a short beard that has already started to turn white. I am so indifferent to him.

Time goes on and he won't mention what happened at school.

'Why did you come just now?' I provoke him.

'The school called me about Marco's little stunt,' he answers calmly, 'but it's all right, don't worry, I've paid for the damage'.

'I'm not worried about the money, but about what he did. Aren't you?' I snap.

'They are boys after all,' he says blithely, playing it down. 'Sometimes they need to let off steam'.

'He was a boy when he slashed your girlfriend's tyres, wasn't he?' I push. 'But you weren't so understanding, then. It's all so much easier from a distance, isn't it? Just write a cheque.'

I kick an empty beer can; there are several on the ground where we are now, leftovers of night-time excursions not yet cleared up. It irritates me that the historic heart of the city should present itself like this to this sort of deserter.

'I don't understand why you dislike her so much,' he utters, downcast. 'You don't even know her.'

With some difficulty, I swallow the answer rising to my lips. Like insane caged tigers, we're on our third lap of the square, and I am not walking away. He irritates me but I continue by his side, trapped by a long, loose chain of shared affections, simultaneous and different. We both loved Olivia, little Marco, my mother's soothing presence. Only the memory of those years ties us together still, not the furious, despondent teenager of today.

Outside the Church of the Blessed Souls Roberto finally stops for a few minutes, fascinated by its façade.

'I didn't remember it so beautiful,' he marvels.

'Many appreciate it more now, since we nearly lost it. You can go in if you want,' I suggest.

He tip-toes through the entrance and holds the door open for me, so I follow him out of politeness. There is too much light, and in place of incense a whiff of new concrete, from the partition wall separating this small accessible area from the rest. The usual nausea forces me out, but I don't immediately understand what's brought it on. He follows me, disappointed by what little is left inside.

He suggests a coffee and I thank him, perhaps next time.

'Anyway, Marco plays football every Saturday afternoon, in a field on the way to Pile. You could go over there when you're free,' I suggest. He nods and walks with me part of the way back to the car.

Under the porticos of the Massimo Cinema, posters are still up for the film showing on Saturday 4th and Sunday 5th April 2009; nobody ever removed them from the dusty notice board. The actors' faces pale below the title, bleached by the sun that reaches through the columns at certain times of day.

I reach the car park and, keys in my hand, I remember where I experienced the same damp smell of fresh masonry that upset me in the church: at the cemetery, the day of the funerals.

10

I fell sick for Roberto in the first year of upper secondary school, the guy who always failed maths and was the most talented at the Casella Conservatoire that he attended at the same time. He was sometimes kind to me, especially when I passed him a copy of the geometry test, then he'd be listless and distant once more, as if he regretted giving too much of himself away. Olivia supported me as she always did, suggesting infallible strategies to win him over, and later tending to half my wounds. In third year I swore to her I didn't care about him any more.

One afternoon of the following year I saw them snogging in a recess of the San Bernardino's staircase. I was running down the stairs to go and study at a friend's house, and Olivia had said something similar at home. We would go back to the village on the evening bus. I stopped for a moment, along with my breath, and thought how strange for her, such a banal place, like everybody else. I walked on, slow and dazed, one step after the other to the thundering of my heart.

They hadn't seen me; they wouldn't have seen anyone in the world. Only then did I remember some of Roberto's looks, when I was talking to my sister in the school corridors. They would go right through me and land on her, as if licking her all over. And once, when we went to one of his first concerts, Olivia's enthusiastic hug at the end had left him speechless and soft, as if just after an orgasm.

The morning after my discovery, I became unable to bear the sight of the nape of his neck at the desk in front. My twin fingers were still there, the thumb on the ear, the others caressing the perfectly symmetrical hairline I knew so well. I moved on a pretext and did not pass him the maths test. Mine had been poor too, though.

Olivia didn't tell me right away and I had time to prepare. When she asked me if I minded I lied, calmly shook my head no and she pretended to believe me. I rolled with the blow, it was hard. But underneath all that I did understand him, Roberto. Olivia had all the powers. Unless they had a chance to protect themselves, animals and humans of both sexes were enchanted. Cats followed her nimbly in the street, backs arched and tails in the air. Dogs trotted after her. When she sprinkled breadcrumbs on the windowsill in the kitchen, sparrows would come to peck at her fingertips.

When Olivia was pregnant, one evening Roberto took us to his maternal grandparents' house in Capestrano, their native village. After dinner we went down the back steps into his childhood garden and we crossed it in silence. It was dark, and an intense scent of thick, sweet petals reached us occasionally from invisible distances. The river was not far, the air rising from it dense with pollen; the hamlet's festival in the background, near yet distant, almost unreal. Suddenly, dozens of fireflies appeared among the grass and the almond trees, as in response to a mysterious command. They flew quietly, barely touching the leaves. They would blend into the darkness for an instant and right away light their magical abdomens again, elsewhere already but only just, shedding light on a bush here, a spider-web there, perhaps the rough skin of a toad near the ditch. We stepped on a field of moving stars, like a fallen sky. Roberto looked on silently, standing behind Olivia, his hand on her seven-month belly, his breath in her ear. I could feel the friction of the shaved chin on my sister's hair, the complex rhythm of his life running through her back to the baby. In the musician's closed mouth started an uncertain hum, a melody read off the stave suspended above the lawn, where notes playfully turned themselves off and moved aside to avoid capture. For the two of them it was a long perfect hour. I had never felt so out of place.

When I least expect them, memories bite me with treacherous teeth. Here, for example, in the waiting room of the orthopaedics department. They are our small departed delights, I look at them from afar and I regret them. They made me weak for what came later, the tremors found me defenceless, my side slender and exposed.

The impatient-sounding nurse must have called my name several times. Finally, I hear her and go. The technician on duty is the same who was there on the day of the accident. We smile and he's friendly and familiar.

'Has your nephew learned to keep his shoes tidy?' he asks as he begins to unravel the bandages.

'No, I've learned to turn the light on when I get up at night.'

He comments with a little laugh and gently removes the slightly yellowed plaster. 'Don't tell me you managed to paint your ceramics.'

'No way. I tried with my left hand too, but it didn't want to know.'

'Now you can make up for lost time,' and he's removing bandages, splint and cotton wool. Instinctively I bend the finger, I can't quite push it all the way. He looks over and nods. 'Well done, try again. Does it hurt?'

'A little, when I get to a certain point.'

'It's normal, don't worry. Luckily you don't need it to hold the brush.'

I notice only now that he has a cold and that he's sniffling continuously. From time to time he blows his nose and afterwards, his hands are damp on my skin. He lines up a few resounding sneezes; the soggy paper can no longer contain the overflowing snot and he rummages in the pockets of his chalk-streaked coat to no avail. I hand him a clean tissue.

The light outside dims suddenly. I rest my palms on the table, under the neon light, and compare the two middle fingers to see if the right one is swollen. He stands up and looks at me silently. Then, with the tip of his index finger, he strokes my liberated digit right up to the nail with a pressure that feels too light to be therapeutic. I slip back along the surface with a frictional whistle, and reclaim my hands. All that's left, for just an instant, is a barely noticeable trail of sweat on the white surface. The technician's shift is over, he declares, and he invites me for an aperitif at the hospital bar. My answer is monosyllabic, I don't even know myself if it's a yes or a no. Still, we walk a stretch of corridor together on the way to the changing room, and as we step softly on the blue linoleum his phlegmy voice admits: 'Yesterday I saw your name on this morning's patient list, and I swapped shifts so I would be here. Wait for me, I'll change and be back in two minutes.'

I smile a sort of goodbye while he disappears trustingly beyond a door.

When I get back to the workshop my hand shakes a little, afraid it won't able to hold a brush again after being idle all this time.

11

In the last few days I have painted non-stop, to catch up on the back-log of work. After a few hours I feel the creaking of my vertebrae when I rotate my head to loosen up the painful tension in my neck. I have burnt a lot of wood in the stove, fingers need to be warm to maintain control of fine movements. As I fed the fire, a splinter, two or three millimetres long, entered my thumb and stayed there, under the skin, undisturbed. In the evening my mother refused to tease it out with a needle – she felt weird about it, and I couldn't manage by myself. I didn't ask Marco; I was worried he'd run me through with one of his abrupt twitches. It isn't a good time for my hands, but they paint willingly here, in the warmth and bright light of the large room. Steam rises from the old saucepan I keep on the stove's cast-iron top to keep the air humid; some mornings I leave orange peel or rosemary twigs next to it, to scent the air.

Even though the owner of the house lives in Bologna, post is still delivered here. When I hear the postwoman's Fiat Panda, the same one every time, braking on the gravel in the drive, I go out to say hello. If she sees I am free, Lucia will tell me some anecdotes from her thankless job – so she says, but with a smile. She talks of the man who sets the dogs on her, apparently in jest, but not so much, whenever she delivers him a speeding fine, or the little old lady who lives alone, who has pasta and potatoes ready when she calls at eleven in the morning, in the hope they might eat together.

The pieces for the Christmas markets are ready now. As I was starting to load them today, the owner of the house arrived and insisted on helping me, without even going inside first. He remembered my immobilised hand from his last visit, and said that it was too early to strain it. I had packed the objects into cardboard boxes of various sizes, and by optimising the space he managed to fit them into the boot. I dropped a box while handing it to him, we both bent over to pick it up and I met his green eyes across the top. I had never seen them so close up.

'Might something have broken?' he asked, concerned.

'I don't think so but I'll check now.' I removed the sticky tape and unwrapped sheets of old papers. The professor watched me examine the bird series Christmas baubles one at a time, rotating them this way and that.

'Nothing broken, thankfully.' I smiled at him.

'Don't take them away, these ones, I'll have them for friends in Bologna.' A spur-of-the-moment idea.

'But you already got some for them last year!' I firmly protested.

'The designs were different. And they asked for more themselves, they want to collect them,' he insisted.

'Then you've earned yourself a discount.'

'No, not this time. You have worked with a sore hand. But I will accept a free one, for me.'

'Do you really like them?' I asked suspiciously.

'I think they are extraordinary. You manage to paint them feeling cold, or hungry, or about to fly away. This one, for example ...'

'The dunnock on the oak branch ...'

'Here, the dunnock looks cold, his feathers a little ruffled, agitated, while this one ...'

'The great tit ...' I suggested, vaguely embarrassed.

'The great tit is sated and resting, her gullet full of grain.'

We went on like that for a bit, me naming the birds and him describing the intention behind their song and the mood of the linnet, the house finch, the nuthatch. Suddenly the chilly shade from the house was over us, with the speed of a winter sunset. We closed up the box and he lifted it in his arms, to take it safely indoors.

There is too much room for our lean stalls, huddled together to face the cold and to comfort each other. This is nothing compared to the markets of years past – traders no longer come from neighbouring regions, not from Naples, even. Not since the earthquake. There are few people around, who knows if more will come later. We see some on the *corso*, striding to the reopened Nurzia bar where they'll have a hot drink, naturally with a piece of Nurzia Brothers nougat; not to be confused with that of the better-known sisters of the same name. The buttoned-up pedestrians walk straight ahead, with only a distracted glance at this little clump of lights and colours that we are, in the middle of the square. There are various crafts – from wooden toys to felted wool bags, my ceramics – but the smells come from the truffled cheese and *mortadella* from Campotosto.

Marco walks right past me with Rash and two other boys, talking eagerly as he does with them, his hands in the pockets of the too-short jacket revealing a strip of candid skin over the low waistline of his shapeless trousers. I shiver just looking at him. He turns to me, swinging curls haloing his head, and we silently exchange a complicit look. He knew he'd find me here. In an instant he's checked on his aunt and the stall, and disappeared off on those skinny legs of his.

I had not been expecting Teresa. She has resurfaced, almost a ghost, from the first few years of secondary school, always at the desk next to Olivia's. After our finals she left L'Aquila to continue her studies elsewhere, and was never seen again. Her father had been an infantry colonel, transferred from town to town. She walks up to me, poised, her lower lip blanched by the small greyish teeth tilted towards the back of her mouth, her shoulders strained. She knows then, perhaps she hasn't known long. When we disentangle from a long tight hug, tears hang from her eyes, without falling. When she tries to say something, I sense her pain in her bitter breath.

'She's left you on your own ...' she whispers.

'No, I live with Marco, her son. And my mother.'

'I still can't quite believe it. She seemed immortal.'

A woman under a fur hat leaves for a moment her friend's arm to come and ask me about a spoon rest with a carrot design, or better still two, crossed over. No, I'm sorry, I hadn't thought of such an original decoration. Shame, she says, she wanted one for her sister-in-law.

'What's he like? Does he look like her?' Teresa starts over, stroking the baubles hanging from their metal supports.

'Marco, you mean ... If you'd got here five minutes earlier you would have seen him. He's sixteen, he has his mother's hair and eyes, the same coffee-coloured birthmark on his left arm. When he's thinking he raises only the one eyebrow, like her, do you remember?'

Of course she remembers. She would have kissed the ground Olivia trod on. She lived, enchanted, in the light of her splendour. She'd come home with us from school on the bus, and after lunch she basked in her company, with the excuse of doing homework. That would happen at least two or three times a week. My sister didn't mind, Teresa was never pushy; she was satisfied just to be there, in her orbit, to comply with her wishes without demanding any attention for herself. When Olivia said anything, even to me or our mother, she would stare at her lips and move her own the same way without making a sound, as with a revelation to

57

be committed to memory. And if she became aware on some afternoon that she was not welcome, she would set herself aside, still in the same room, happy to breathe the same air as the other. I didn't mind her either – she wasn't taking anything away from me, she wasn't worth being jealous of. She was a harmless figurine, lost in her innocent, secret love. I thought I was the only one to see it, so disguised it was in friendly intimacy, hidden in everyday gestures that revealed nothing to Olivia. Teresa would put her arm around her shoulders when looking something up in a book, tuck away a lock of hair that had fallen over the page. She got away with her innocent tender gestures by forgetting to bring her own school books, with a frequency that even I found embarrassing, when, stretched on my bed, I watched them from behind.

My mother would reassure hers, who often phoned to apologise on behalf of her daughter and invite Olivia to theirs, at least once in a while. But the girls felt uncomfortable in the military atmosphere of that home. My sister did consent to lunch there a few times, to escape immediately afterwards.

'His father, does he see him?' Teresa's voice brings me back. She knows it's Roberto but will not name him, the boy who suddenly stole her afternoons with Olivia, leaving her only the meagre contact during school hours, or little more.

'Yes, he sees him. Roberto lives in Rome but comes often, whenever his commitments allow. You know, he holds concerts all over Europe and even in Japan …. But he calls Marco every day, when he's abroad. And he takes the boy with him in the summer.'

Teresa seems surprised by the passion in my response. I am surprised myself, the lie found its way to my mouth like the unexpected regurgitation of a greasy, indigestible food. I have defended Roberto from an inexistent attack, materialised perhaps out of my own rage against him, a pale reflection of Marco's own. I have protected him as if he were still one of the family, a brother you're always squabbling with but are ready to shed blood for, should he be hit by one other than yourself.

Some well-intentioned browsers come close; I immediately recognise those who intend to buy. In an instant I wrap some red tissue paper around the Christmas bauble Teresa touched with the most interest, and place it in her hand. She understands she has to go, now.

12

1. You must take care of the dog because it's YOURS.
2. The dog is NEVER allowed in the bedrooms.
3. YOU must deal with the dog's meals, but not in the morning or you'll miss the bus.
4. YOU will take the dog out, even when it's raining.
5. The dog is NEVER allowed on the sofa, NOT EVEN when it's just the two of you at home.
6. The dog must at all times sleep in his basket ON THE BALCONY.

A woman from the next platform crosses the square of uncultivated ground that separates us, always the same route, one way and then the other. She has carved a path where weeds no longer grow, stamped out by her obsessive steps. She walks chanting through broken teeth, 'L'Aquila bella mia, my beloved, I want to see you again ...' and finishes the traditional rhyme with a shrill wrong note, right on that 'bella mia'.

She knows the life story of everyone here at Coppito Three. She repeats it all aloud to herself, so she won't forget, as inquisitive as an insatiable rodent. They say she was not like this, before the earthquake. At the beginning I was almost a little scared of her, I'd try to avoid her when I saw her from a distance, the grey unkempt hair and randomly assembled clothes. Now I always ask her how she is, and she answers 'well, a little, and bad, a little,' the syllables twisting in her mouth. Then she gives me a little nudge and tells me something about someone, but I often don't understand what, about whom.

I run into her one afternoon at the front door and she bursts out, 'Very sweet, your nephew's dog.' I leave the bags of shopping and walk to the corner she's pointing to with her hairy chin. Flattened behind a pillar, I watch open-mouthed the mysterious intimacy between man and beast. There they are, sitting on the new cement. Or rather, Marco is sitting cross-legged, while out of the half-opened zip of his jacket pokes the affectionate head of a quadruped, a Volpino perhaps, held tight to his ribs. Next to them is an old plastic bowl full of water and, perfectly cleaned out of any trace of food, the plate that cracked a few days ago when I let it slip from my wet hands. It had been hanging around at home until he said, with unexpected zest: 'Best throw this away before it breaks and cuts someone.'

Over the last week, I hadn't been able to explain to myself Marco's strange comings and goings. He'd go downstairs straight after lunch, his padded jacket slightly puffier on the left side, and I'd see him from the window, twisting sideways as he walked so as not to show that side. On every third step he'd look up, with a surly and guilty glance at the eyes he felt on him. He'd turn the corner and wouldn't come back for hours. When questioned about the food frequently disappearing from the fridge, he'd snap: 'You're always going on about me not eating and now you complain if I get hungry and have a snack?'

The dog worships him, ears lowered. At one point, unable to contain itself, it licks the pimples within tongue's reach, as if they were swollen with honey. Marco laughs and pretends to pull back, but only for an instant, worried the dog might take his sudden rejection to heart. They belong to each other already, it's too late to separate them. They each know what devotion looks like.

A stiffness fractures inside me, the metal bar drawn across my chest to support it from the inside. I don't show myself. I pull back, pick up the shopping at the door and with some effort go up the stairs, steeper and more numerous than usual. Celery stalks poke through the handles of the plastic bag and tickle my wrist; my mother will use them in a vegetable broth. But first I will talk to her, to persuade her. It isn't difficult, when it's about Marco.

A few days later, he goes out on the balcony and almost trips over the dog basket bought by me and his grandmother, together with two coloured bowls and a few other doggy knick-knacks. He gets back in, his curls exploding into a halo, and stares at us gasping, dumbfounded. I dictate the iron rules with a tone attempting to sound inflexible, but my mother can't repress a smile.

'Now go and get it,' I tell him at the end of my lecture. He returns in an instant with the little mutt, so he calls it, in his arms. He brings it close to us, first to one and then the other, in a brief round of introductions. When he brings it close to me, the little beast seems to sense a threat and barricades its trembling self inside the uncertain fortress of its black fur. I hint at stretching a hand to lightly brush its head and the dog blinks, neck retreating into its shoulders as if to duck an imminent blow.

'Try with something to eat, perhaps he won't be so afraid,' Marco suggests and I obediently comply, but when I reach for the bowl he adds: 'No, no, give him a little meat with your hand.'

I kneel down and the dog is lowered to the floor, to balk at the mouthful I am offering. For a few long minutes desire for food struggles with fear of the unknown. Marco is two steps away, leaning his back against the wall, observing us in silence. The dog is about to give up, drops its head and pulls back a little, then becomes interested once more. I leave a bit of food on the floor and pull back myself. It pricks up its ears and looks at me. It's reassured, I can be trusted.

On our request, the Veterinary Service supply us with the data on the microchip, and more. The vet knows the whole story. Bric is a crossbreed, eight years old, as his already greying whiskers can attest. He'd been adopted as a puppy by a man in Onna, who then died in the earthquake. For months, the dog had kept vigil at the ruins of their house, feeding on a few merciful bones and on the lingering scent of his master. On the night of 6th April he'd warned him in vain of the coming quake, barking and snapping at the sleeve of his pyjamas. In the end the man, exasperated by the dog's agitation, had put him outside and gone back to bed, where he was to die. That was the tale of a surviving neighbour, who had found it difficult to get to sleep in his car after the first tremors earlier that evening. From there, he watched the dog's last efforts to drag his owner out of the door. When he finally came to terms with his loss, Bric started to wander the countryside, and arrived one afternoon at our C.A.S.E., to Marco.

Not for a single night does he get to watch the stars from his basket, we fear the cold for him (in violation of rule number six). Each one of us finds more or less irrational pretexts to keep him indoors – he is nearly old, he has suffered a lot, he might disturb the neighbours. So he sleeps on a dog mat, in a corner. Every now and then he startles and quivers with that pitiful tremor of his, howling under his breath in unknown tongues, just as his darling next door talks in his sleep like one possessed. Every night Marco, who is the last one to bed, carelessly leaves his bedroom door ajar (in violation of rule number two). When I point that out to him, he innocently maintains that there is something wrong with the handle.

'I swear, aunt, I don't forget. It's just that at night something gets loose in the mechanism, sometimes I hear a click in my sleep.'

At dawn Bric nuzzles that narrow invitation wider, and places his front paws on the bed. He could do that earlier, unbeknown to us, but he resists solitude and separation for a few tolerable hours instead. He waits for a sliver of external light before re-joining his master. He stands there for a few instants, in ecstasy, his damp nostrils dilated to receive the foul breath of the other, then joyfully licks the sleeping face. So every morning Marco wakes up laughing, and when his grandmother comes across the dog wandering around the flat, even in the rooms forbidden to him, she noiselessly whispers, 'bless you'.

13

I go into the Red Zone, the second time in the space of a few months. It's snowing lightly, whirls of delicate snowflakes unwilling to settle on the already-fallen mantle. I tread cautiously where no one has yet been, with a noise like walking on compressed polystyrene. A brief stop at San Pietro's church, as close as the supports allow. The bells have been removed from the parvis. I know they'd been laid here, mouths facing down, they were here for quite a while. Perhaps disturbed by my arrival, a crow takes flight from a balcony, almost elegant in his dark suit. The grey pattern of cracks on the façades has turned into irregular white garlands, and it is through those fractures in the plastering that the weather seeps in. A small car is parked right up against a wall, windscreen and bonnet are caved in though the wall is still intact. I look up to see where the rubble fell from. When I do, snowflakes catch on my eyelashes and I see the missing roof through starred crystals, which soon melt and drip into my eyes. Two-toned seats are visible through the car door, open wide, and the airbag, having inflated in vain, now hangs collapsed from the steering wheel. It must have parked there on the evening of 5th April, the way that those of us who lived in the old town centre used to park every day, automatically, with the same manoeuvres, only a few millimetres from the wall so as not to obstruct the traffic through streets that were always too narrow.

I end up in a square amplified by whiteness and silence. I don't recognise it right away under the snowfall from the low, invisible sky. The buildings along its perimeter are closed in on their inner darkness. There is no smoke coming out of chimneys, no cooking smells. The weather is perfect for soft polenta and a rich sausage stew, thickening slowly on the stove and steaming up the windows. The transparent plastic sheets that had replaced the shattered glass have ripped, blown by the wind.

I cross the perfect expanse and then turn back to face my lonely footsteps, the impermanent and irregular line showing me the way I have come. With the side of my palm I gather the superficial layer from a wall and savour the metallic taste of unknown heights. I walk on towards a monotone sound, perhaps shutters banging to the beat of the rushing wind. This time I don't avoid Via del Drago: that's where I'm headed. Before I reach number 28, where Olivia and Marco used to live, I review the death count of the buildings and note how the numbers decrease regularly by a single unit, three, two, one. My one, Olivia. I come to a breathless stop outside her house. Footprints head right here from the opposite side of the road, and then leave again. One set, already filling with fresh snow. Someone has come, they must have gone in, without hesitation, you can see a half print in the snow, with the front half already across the threshold. He then came out again, without turning back – the line of reversed footprints is neat and straight, like the one going in. I stupidly touch the padlock on the front door, as if it could possibly have retained the heat of the hands that opened it and then closed it again. An hour or more must have passed from that visit, I try and calculate. I improvise myself a detective and guess the difference between the footsteps going in and out to understand how long the intruder spent inside. Not long, perhaps he only needed to pick something up. The shoes, so big, probably the same size as Marco's. I know nothing of his day, I barely saw him this morning. A simple look, if too direct, is enough to irritate him when he's just out of bed. I can't imagine what outlandish reasons might have brought him here.

In a sheltered corner of their first-floor balcony, hanging on the washing line, is the *Simpsons* sweatshirt he'd asked of me for his last Christmas here. I remember the picture on the front, Homer standing in front of a barbecue with KISS THE CHEF printed across his stained T-shirt. I hadn't been able to find it anywhere and in the end I decided to go to Rome for it; I made the trip specially. Marco ripped the paper off and was moved almost to tears by his yellow hero, so much so that he rewarded me with a noisy kiss, preceded by the blinding mass of his hair.

'Nobody here in L'Aquila has this one yet,' he announced, proud of it, proud of me too.

From where I stand I can make out the big bald head pointing down and the arm stretched towards steaks that haven't yet fallen after three years, nearly four, upside down. Just as the sweatshirt itself won't fly away, frozen into allegiance to its balcony. One of the pegs is gone and so it hangs lopsided, like so much else in the town. The sleeves would be too short for Marco now, they'd barely cover his elbows and his waist would be bare up to his ribs. A sharp pain rises to my nose. It must be the cold, or obstructed tears.

A dull and muffled thud at the end of the street, it sounds like something collapsing, something small, perhaps a cornice or part of a loft giving way under the weight of the snow. Nobody would know, if I weren't here. Perhaps I'm wrong, there are other ghosts stealthily wandering these streets, in the dark as well, their flashlights pointed at the cobblestones ahead of their feet. Some people secretly sleep in their class-E homes, even, so as not to leave them feel abandoned. They wait to rebuild. I know someone who does that – he said it's okay, you can trust the people who secured the buildings.

'It will go to ruin if I don't go every day,' he told me of his inhabitable home. I feared for his sanity.

The only officially remaining resident is an old writer, almost a hero. After the tremor he remained in his flat, which had suffered little damage. When the men from Civil Protection turned up to rescue him, he pretended to follow them out of the door, his suitcase in his hand, with his old-fashioned courteous manner. He locked the door behind them and nobody dared enforce the evacuation order. He called two builders for the most urgent repairs and has continued to live there, at first without electricity and gas, and still without neighbours. He writes and slowly ages, among his cats, his dusty books, his unending studies. He strolls to a restaurant that has now reopened, where he eats with his few remaining teeth.

There will be other collapses when the snow melts, I think. Overnight the water that has penetrated the walls expands as it freezes, and the cracks widen. L'Aquila is drenched and bloated, after all this time. The rain has soaked in right down to the foundations, infiltrating between brick and brick. Marco shouldn't come here, it's dangerous. I'll change the padlock tomorrow; he must have managed to get a copy of the key. I squeeze the one in my pocket, and decide against letting myself in. It's almost dark by now, suddenly, with no twilight, like on the moon.

My telephone vibrates. 'And why aren't you home yet, what are you waiting for, in this weather?' my mother asks, worried.

'Don't worry, I'll be there soon. Is Marco back?'

'Just now, soaked from head to toe. Toes especially, his shoes are dripping.'

I would like to ask if they're dripping with the snow he walked on in Via del Drago, in front of his house. I hurry

68

back, down one alleyway and then another, retracing my disappearing steps in reverse, and when I get to the Bright Fountain I find the army vehicles set out in a circle, like giant turtles clothed in white.

14

When he knocks on the car window I jump out of my skin. The camouflage uniform with a rifle hanging from his shoulder is talking to me, and I can't hear. With the slanted barrel of his weapon he motions for me to lower the window, how silly of me. I comply and also take off my hood. The voice reaches me now, ensconced in mist, vaguely ironic.

'Where have you been in this weather?'

'Oh, just around ...' I try to answer, intimidated.

'In this weather?' he repeats doubtfully, raising his highbrows. I can't quite place his accent on the map of Northern Italy.

'I didn't go far ...' I justify myself.

'Didn't you see the barriers?' he asks. He even points them out to me, again with the same implement.

'I didn't go through.' I find myself lying demurely, but then I look straight into his apathetic deep-set eyes, and discard any uneasiness. 'Don't you know another way of indicating? Just now you nearly pointed your rifle at me, to ask me to lower my window.'

'No need to worry, the safety latch is on,' he responds with a glance at his weapon. He stands on wide-open legs, his sex prominent inside the khaki trousers. I continue to shift him back and forth along the arc of the Alps, down to the plain, searching for where he came from.

'I should think so. In any case, those of us who don't carry weapons use our fingers to point, the index finger to be precise. Indicate comes from index.'

'You haven't told me why you came here yet. This isn't exactly a place for strolls.' This time, he uses his jaw and an expressionless glance to indicate the deserted slice of imprisoned town.

'I was looking for my nephew.'

'Wandering around on this lovely day too, is he? What's he like? I might have seen him,' he insists while the snow falls implacably on him.

'Never mind, he called from home not long ago. If that's all, I'd like to go home too.'

'Off you go then,' he agrees, shifting his weight on the other leg. 'But be more careful next time. Your footprints come from inside the Red Zone to your car. It's forbidden to go in, it says on the signs.'

Only now I spot another like him a little further on, seeking refuge from the snow under the bus shelter, stamping his combat boots on the ground. I start the engine with a grimace, while the heating refuses to come to life. I crawl behind the flashing light of a snowplough to the first junction. My mother phones again. I reassure her.

When I get back it's no longer snowing; everything is freezing around the C.A.S.E.

I find Marco stretched out on the sofa. His grandmother has managed to settle him down with a blanket after the chill he caught. But those long skinny toes are peeping out at the end, bare. On the floor, the empty mug with the cow design front and back, a dusty trail of cocoa witness to the hot chocolate drunk to the benefit of his acne. He has no chocolate moustaches at the sides of his mouth, he must have wiped them with his hand. Nor does his face show any sign of a visit to Via del Drago. He's reading a comic, relaxed and composed; every now and then he reaches out to stroke the dog snoozing happily on the rug. For a moment he takes his eyes off the page and looks my way, without turning his head. I see myself through those sly, secretive eyes as someone easily taken for a ride. I look back, straight and confident. It was him, the one who went into his house.

'Where did you go?' I explore, cautiously.

'L'Aquilone, with Rash and the others. That's where we go when it's bad weather.' The lie tumbles out instinctive and casual: he's sure to have practised on his grandmother. And they do go, I have seen them there sometimes.

'Without any money?'

'You don't have to buy anything. We meet there, we wander around, look at the shop windows. It's where we meet.'

'The shopping centre?' I question with mild surprise.

'Yes, the shopping centre. Why not? Where do you expect us to go? If you can suggest anywhere else ...' he starts to get heated.

'No, no, fine. If it suits you ...'

'Where else? There is nowhere else during the day. And you, where have you been in this weather?' he fights back.

'At the workshop, as always,' I say, hanging my head. I pretend to scratch a cheekbone to cover my blush.

'It's hard to believe that from your soaking shoes,' doubts the expert.

I follow the direction of his scepticism. Even though I wiped them on the mat, my shoes are now yielding to the warm floor the snow packed into the tread of the rubber soles, drop by drop. In an instant Marco has deflated me, I don't know what to say. He concentrates back on his comic, while I mop up two 36-size puddles with a rag.

I'm not finished yet. I make up an excuse for my mother and go down to the car. I sit in the dark interior and phone Roberto. He answers under the sudden burden of my fluorescent name calling him back to the shrouded part of his life.

I tell him I want him to come to ours for a meal, one of these days. Yes, I'm sure, I'll prepare the ground. It won't be easy, I know, but it's necessary. We need him here, there are things going on I don't understand. Marco secretly goes back to the partially collapsed house, and it's dangerous. No, I didn't see him, but I am sure. I don't know what he might be doing there, does his father have any idea? We agree in the end, that we'll talk again soon. I hang up, two icicles under my armpits, a sigh of relief in my mouth.

It's only the slow, hesitant movement that betrays the figure in the darkness that contains it – the lights must have burnt out. Everything frightens me today, but it's only an instant. I immediately recognise the slight outline of our neighbour, and I catch up with her on our way out of the car park. I can't understand what she was doing under my platform; I walk with her to hers.

'Where are you coming from in this freezing cold?' I ask her softly.

'From the cemetery,' she answers simply, and the moon floods her face with white.

'Isn't it closed now?'

'Yes, I just walk around it, that's all. I'm there in the morning. At this time I only go to say goodnight to her.'

'So every night …'

'Yes. Is it very cold, do you think?'

'Well, yes … Don't you feel it?'

'It's always cold for me. I worry about the little one, though she is well covered. Do you think it's colder here, or at the cemetery?'

'Here, surely, we're more exposed to the wind. It's more sheltered over there, and then there's the wall all around.'

'Ah, better like that …. Your mother said the same.'

On cue, the freshly fallen snow, still light on the ground, is blown over us by a gust of wind. Instinctively I put my arm around her shoulders, to make sure she doesn't fly away. With a slight pressure I steer her away from the wind. She's so docile. When I say goodbye I gently stroke the bundle of her hair, as dry as Olivia's lock inside my flower-paper box.

15

I was already scared, on the night of 5th April. My mother heard it on the telephone. Come and sleep here, at the village, she said. Then I asked her if she was scared, pretending to misunderstand her. No, she wasn't, not until it stole her daughter; until then, she was prepared to add the persisting tremors to the long list of adversities she had lived through, like the snow of '56 that left them without bread, or the bout of pneumonia in '82 that just wouldn't go away. The earthquake would not be healed, either, it was a deep epilepsy in the earth that had struck suddenly and wouldn't come to an end. It had been convulsing under our feet for months with no recognisable pattern, no regularity, at times more intense, at others barely perceptible, in a disorderly and unnerving sequence. Occasionally, a longer pause would fool us into believing the latest tremor would be the last, until the next one, stronger still.

At night I would listen to the faint scratching of nails against the sheets, to every breath, and to a sort of moaning inside the thickness of the walls, sporadic and weak. I'd struggle to fall asleep in a home occupied by invisible tensions, creakings, sudden crumblings between the bricks of the cross-vaulted ceiling. Some mornings I'd find small mounds of coarse dust here and there, fallen from above, and before cleaning up I'd pinch some between my fingers and look up to compare the colour with that of the plaster up there. I could have got by on just a couple of hours' rest from the slithering anguish, every day a short free interval when nothing at all could happen. Instead, the seismic swarm would hit at random and, if I craved a pause in my perpetual alert, since by then it was spring-time, I'd go and spend an afternoon at the Sun Park, to doze off with my back to a tree trunk. Sitting over the titan imprisoned by geological layers, I'd wait for it to shudder, curious and safe for a time in the rarefied silence. It never happened, when I was there. The restless giant was sleeping too.

Olivia phoned after the strong tremor at eleven that night, pretending to be worried.

'Come,' she said. 'I can't move; I have to wait for Marco.'

He'd gone for a pizza with friends, then they'd run outside, like everybody else, and didn't want to get back indoors too soon.

'You come now though, I don't want to be alone,' she repeated.

She was well acquainted with my fear. More cunning and subtle than our mother, she had reversed our roles to give me an excuse to reach her and release myself into her protection. I put my jacket on and went – my toothbrush was already in my handbag. It'd take less than ten minutes on foot, cutting through the alleyways. I walked down the middle, away from projecting ledges. I heard voices, as I got closer to the centre. There were people in the street, but not for the Palm Sunday celebrations, not for one last drink before turning in to prepare for work on Monday. When I reached the *corso* I was caught in the wave of general confusion. I walked on, a woman bumped into me without apologising, a boy dropped a coin from his pocket while pulling out his phone. It sounded heavy, perhaps a two Euro coin, but he didn't bother to pick it up. Shreds of conversations brushed over me, someone mentioned Giuliani who had anticipated a high-magnitude tremor with his radon studies, over at Sulmona, though. Many were undecided between their beds at home and the reclining seats of their cars for what was left of the night. There was no wind but a sort of breeze, quite cold. Most of the people had stayed indoors, we had been reassured. The earthquake was exhausting its energy in the low-intensity swarm; it would have no energy left for a destructive event.

Olivia opened the door and then sat down again at the desk in the corner, the lamplight shining on lined foolscap sheets. She was correcting her pupils' Latin homework, in the last few hours of her life.

'Sorry, I'll finish this and then I'm done. I don't know how, but this one managed to copy the version off the Internet,' she said.

Unlike the previous day, the large rectangular table was no longer in the middle of the room. Olivia had pushed it against the bearing wall, perhaps after the eleven o'clock tremor. On top, neatly stacked, a full backpack, a folded blanket, a flashlight, keys and mobile phone.

She finished her work; I saw her write on the back of the sheet with a red pen. She had folded the assignments she'd already marked into a text book, and the others were stacked with her pen on top, waiting for her. She turned the light off and came towards me. I pointed to the table with a nervous look.

'If we really have to, we're ready to run. We can take cover under there, and when it stops we pick up those few bits and we're off. Don't worry, you heard the engineer who checked the buildings, they've resisted far worse earthquakes.'

'When is Marco coming back?'

'He arrived two minutes before you and went straight to bed. He fears nothing, that son of mine. But best keep the bedroom doors open.' She went to do that with Marco's.

'Where do you want to sleep?' she asked with a smile. 'In the big bed with your little sister, perhaps?' and she ruffled my hair.

'Silly … the sofa's fine, it's big and comfortable. I'll just take a quilt, we'll sleep with our clothes on, won't we?'

'That's a bit over the top, you're not getting ready for the end of the world. Marco's in his underwear in his room, he didn't even bother with pyjamas.'

'As silly as his mother.'

'Never mind, how about a night cap? Warm milk or *limoncello*?'

Warm milk, we drank it sitting close to each other, in silence, with the television turned down to minimum.

'Aren't you going to bed?' I asked.

'Yes, in a minute.'

Instead, she put her drink down and took her glasses off, and after a few minutes she slid slowly along the back of the sofa, her already sleeping head finding a cushion. I pulled her legs across my own and covered her. Later, when I wanted to sleep too, I carefully slipped in behind her, finding a space that was narrow, but soft and warm. At one point she gathered herself in an almost foetal position, and I wrapped my whole body round her, folding myself to reproduce the same lines as hers, in a re-enactment of our uterine position as I used to imagine it when I was little. I put my arm around her, only the right one. In the rhythm of her heartbeat I felt an unconscious contentment fill her heart.

I don't know how long I kept vigil on her last sleep. At an uncertain time I pulled myself away, put on my jacket and went out on the balcony, as if called by an acute foreboding. The hanging clothes were perfectly still in the darkness. I could make out their half-human outlines, but didn't recognise the Homer Simpson sweatshirt.

The night birds were singing, one in particular would repeat the same monotone '*kew*'. I thought I had recognised the scops owl: Roberto once told us that its song is an E flat major. Before I had the time to wonder what a scops owl could be doing in the town centre, the birds fell silent, all at once. Almost in the same instant the dogs started barking, a chorus expanding in a circle from the blocks of flats and further away, from the countryside and the outlying villages. They were giving warning of what was to come, in their unheeded language. Among the others, Bric's voice in Onna was barking against his master's reluctance, and I didn't know it. Suddenly the air struck me, hard, not wind but a compact mass of blasted air. I bounced back in and it started.

I open my eyes without going further into the 3.32 am of my memory. The earthquake shakes only one shoulder, with skinny hook-like fingers.

'You in that armchair, no point pretending to be asleep. I know it was you.' He takes a step back. His pimples ooze purulent rage and all his curls are pointed at me.

'What are you talking about?' I ask him, instinctively tensing up.

'You changed the padlock to my house. Don't deny it!'

'I am not. But how do you know?'

'That's none of your business. What were you thinking?' The dog has got up from his mat in the corner to come and stand by him, looking from one to the other as we speak, his ears perked up. You can see whose side he's on.

'I found out that someone was going in and out your house, undisturbed, perhaps with a copy of the key, so I changed the padlock.'

'What a genius! But it's nothing to do with you, it's MY house.'

'It's dangerous to go there, the flat is inhabitable. Part of it has collapsed and the whole building is propped up. I'm responsible for you.'

'Really! Responsible for what? I can look after myself, I don't need you. Now give me the key.'

'Not now. We'll talk about this with your father, he's coming here for lunch on Sunday.'

'I bet it was your idea to invite him. You can forget it, I won't be there.' He turns on his heels and Bric trots along behind him to his room, turning back a couple of times to shoot me a reproachful look.

16

He arrives at noon with a cake too big for four people. He hands it to me on the doorstep and I say, come on in. Marco, his back to us, responds to the greeting with a barely audible 'ciao' and doesn't come closer. He's very busy with the keypad of his phone. Just now, when I asked him to go and open the door, he shook his head and pointed to it, pretending to be speaking with someone. He has remained at home against his will, and now he's putting off facing his father.

Roberto takes a few uncertain steps into the room, towards the figure pulling away from the stove. After years he extends his hand and a greeting to his mother-in-law, and she barely grants him her fingertips, for an instant, and a stretch of silence. It doesn't last long. Marco lets the dog in from the balcony and Bric bays at the intruder with the aggressiveness reserved to those invading his territory. I tell him off and he takes no notice, just looks up to the silent face of his master as if asking for confirmation, you tell me if I'm doing the right thing. Finally he calms down and moves to the corner, tail between his legs. He almost curls himself down, then leaps back, growling for a taste of Roberto's clothed ankle. This time I grab him by the collar and drag him outside.

'Training your dog to attack, are you?' I hiss as I brush against Marco, who isn't in the least perturbed.

Roberto plays it down: 'Cute, the Volpino guard dog.' I offer him a prosecco, both aperitif and compensation; I got it specially. My mother refuses with a barely horrified nod, and goes back to her cooking. It seems I'll be the only one to share the wine with him, and I don't even like it. I touch my glass to his. The other two, their attention summoned by the sound, look on disapprovingly. I drink the thimbleful of white in one gulp and it goes down the wrong way.

Marco steals my usual place at the table to avoid sitting in front of his father. The proximity must still feel excessive: he barricades himself behind the unsurmountable barrier of his hair, which affords no view beyond his empty plate. Roberto looks away from his son's spiky head and sighs, uncomfortable. I look for words.

'How are your concerts going?'

'Well, thank you. We'll be in Germany next week, in Dresden, an exchange with the Philharmonic Orchestra.'

But the conversation doesn't take off. The few sounds we have produced bounce against invisible obstacles and roll back, distorted. A powerful resistance is suspended in the air. Perhaps the artichoke timbale will help. I serve my brother-in-law a generous portion, a smaller one to me and Marco; my mother will take care of her own. The reticent cook has surpassed herself. Before it's cut, everyone looks over, from their own side of the table, at the geometrically arranged dish, its hues grading from the medium green of the intermediate layers, to the yellow of the handmade pasta sheets, to the white of the béchamel sauce, overflowing slightly along the sides. For a time the only noise is that of forks and knives at work, in the absence of human voices.

For as long as we chew, the burden of mutual discomfort is bearable but then, in the brief interlude between first and second course, it returns to oppress us.

'A little more timbale?' I suggest to Roberto.

'That was plenty, thank you. Delicious,' he says, turning to my mother, who stands up just in time to side-track the compliment. He torments the slice of bread next to his napkin, pulls a bit off and reduces it to crumbs between his thumb and index finger. After that, he pushes the crumbs this way and that on the tablecloth, and finally gathers them up and kneads them together into a single lump.

Behind me, the oven opens on the dying sizzle of the roast chicken and potatoes, the aroma spreading, rich and spicy. Suddenly I remember that Roberto has been vegetarian for a few years, and I also remember Marco and his grandmother yesterday afternoon, busy plotting today's lunch. My mother and I had forgotten that our guest doesn't eat meat, but Marco hadn't; he must have done it on purpose. I can hear him now, asking for a nice free-range chicken in that tone of his, ingratiating and irresistible.

I find some season vegetables in the fridge, already cooked, reheat them in a pan and serve them to my brother-in-law with an assortment of local cheeses rummaged on the spot. In the meantime his mother-in-law also apologises, through her teeth, for the oversight.

'My memory is starting to fail me ...' she justifies herself, contrite.

'You mustn't worry, the mozzarella is excellent,' Roberto reassures her, perhaps not feeling the ridicule of addressing her again as formally as he used to that first year, when he would come for Olivia on a borrowed moped with a busted muffler. Marco observes unperturbed, for once applying himself earnestly to a chicken leg and then the other, until only two perfectly stripped bones are left on his plate. He has let in the pacified dog and passes him something under the table; Bric licks his greasy fingers before clamping his teeth on the morsel.

'If you give him the cheese crusts you'll make a friend of him,' I suggest to Roberto, pointing to the four-legged beast. Marco glares at me, irritated, and pre-empts his father. 'Here, Bric,' he calls, and lets the dog out again.

'Ah, I was forgetting, I met Irene on the stairs, in Rome, and she asked me to say hello.' Roberto tries again with his son.

'I don't know an Irene,' comes the ill-mannered reply.

'You know, the girl on the third floor …'.

'I don't remember her.'

'He's busy with the local girls now,' comes my mother's surprising intervention, with an attempt at a smile for the guest. She's feeling sorry for him now, I know her. After a moment, though, she reshapes her mouth into its usual sorrowful arc, almost in regret at having conceded too much to the man who abandoned her daughter. 'If he'd stayed with her, she wouldn't have come back to die in L'Aquila,' she once let slip at the cemetery with the flower seller, but in a whisper, as if talking to herself. This is what we accuse Roberto of, inwardly. The three of us all need a scapegoat for this inconceivable loss.

Marco needs his father, too.

The tremor finds him weak and unprepared. He shrieks ohmygod and jumps up, the chair falling backwards. He goes white, and sweat drenches his forehead in an instant. He looks at us quizzical and gasping, one and then the other, hardly believing how calm we are.

'Don't worry, the only good thing about these toy-houses is that they are safe,' I reassure him.

A tinkling of glasses dies down in the display cabinet, and Marco stretches up an arm to still the swinging lampshade.

'Three point two,' he shows off, and scoffing at Roberto: 'You made more noise than the earthquake.'

He stands up, walks around the table that separates them and picks up his father's chair.

'I don't want cake,' he announces dryly on his way to his room.

His father sits down again, mortified and pale. To his apologies his mother-in-law replies, there is no need, we're used to it, he isn't.

'At first we used to react even more than you did,' I confirm. 'If the floor vibrated when a lorry went by we'd think it was a tremor.'

Nobody feels like cake, but we eat it out of reciprocal good manners. Roberto stares impotently at his son's closed door before looking down at the handmade millefeuille from the prestigious Rome pastry shop. The way he holds his mouth, you'd think he's eating bile cream.

Later he doesn't even get to say goodbye. Marco appears to be fast asleep when I go in to see why he isn't responding, but there is something unnatural about his lethargy.

'Shall I wake him up?' I ask, uncertain.

'No, leave him be.'

He can't stay any longer, he has to go. We haven't discussed a single thing concerning the boy; he said he'll call him tomorrow and will try to meet him as soon as possible.

My mother moves slowly and silently as she tidies up, I do the dishes. Later she allows herself a rest on the armchair, laying her head back as if exhausted, hollowed out. Some days age you more than a lifetime. Her cheeks, and her state of mind have fallen in. The construction she has laboriously erected and supported for three years looks on the verge of imploding, destabilised by today's visit. If I get close she hides her hands and the not unnoticeable tremor that stirs them. I borrow her Catholic tongue and ask her if she has managed to forgive him, Roberto.

'God gives me the strength, for Marco's sake,' the Catholic responds, with no enthusiasm. 'If he'd stayed, she wouldn't have come back to die here,' she adds, a reticent bitterness in her voice, repeating the eternal recrimination to herself.

17

She died of her tardiness.

The din had subsided, made more fluid by the undulating motion of the house, which was no longer bouncing. Someone had turned down the speed on the demented mixer that contained us. The floor tiles, lifted by air bubbles, had stopped jumping up, sounding like cheerful ducks. The wall-mounted mirror seemed to have fallen and smashed a long time ago, and the furniture had stopped throwing itself wildly against the walls. Under the table where we had taken refuge the waves were softening, as were the nausea, the dizziness, the sharp pain to the head. The earthquake must have stopped, only inertia seemed to keep us moving. Marco was no longer screaming and for the last few seconds I had stopped feeling as if I were about to fall a long way down. We were there, on our knees, our hands on the floor. Olivia had been hanging on to them for dear life, mine on one side, her son's on the other, trying to balance the alternating thrusts and the suction from below. Only for an instant did she let go of my hand, to stretch her arm up to the wooden tabletop above, feeling and searching among the fallen rubble for the objects left there the previous night. We'd heard them roll here and there over our heads, in the general confusion.

She was the first to leave our shelter. Groping around she found the fallen torch and then, with the help of the beam of light, the blanket, which she draped over Marco's shoulders, the backpack and the keys, which she entrusted to me. Thinking back, she seemed to behave just like a teacher, busy carrying out an evacuation drill, with more gravity than normal. The precarious silence was broken by the intermittent screech of a rope tensed almost to breaking point, the friction of a thousand sharpened teeth somewhere inside the distressed walls, high up. Later, I would understand that it was the main support beam, about to fall. Barely balancing, it was waiting for Olivia.

'We have to go now,' she said. There was no electricity, she shone the flashlight along the path to the stairs through the cluttered floor. Marco, ahead, still barefoot, cried out as he stepped on a piece of broken glass. On the first step she motioned me ahead with a hand on my back and her voice: you go down with him, hurry.

'And you?' I stopped.

'I'll grab a couple of things and I'll be right down, you go with Marco.'

Her son's name was her last word.

The earthquake had blocked the door to the street; the two of us couldn't budge it but we managed to get through a window with no mesh. We emerged into the slowly settling dark dust, me and my nephew in his pants and T-shirt, the blanket over him. We immediately looked up to the balcony that we couldn't make out against the building.

'Why is she taking so long?' Marco shrieked. She was taking the time she needed to find him a pair of trousers and a pair of shoes, the firemen found her like that six hours later, with the long, long jeans next to her open fingers. She had wanted to protect him from the cold and the discomfort of showing himself to others who had escaped the earthquake, his skinny, already hairy legs poking out from under the edge of the woollen blanket. I will never tell him that.

'Come, hurry up,' he screamed at the first floor. Then another short tremor and the crash, inside. He called her

twice, two short sharp barks. I followed his fish-like dart
back through the window, he was climbing the steps without
caring for the rubble biting the soles of his feet. Upstairs,
after a few steps, we fell face down on the rubble. He called
her, again, asked her where she was. His hands grabbed
something too heavy for him to move. Then off in another
direction, blindly, in the darkness, until we found a brick,
two, three, and threw them behind us. I dug with him, and I
called out too, for a long time. In return, no voice, no moan,
no breath. Her name couldn't reach her, under all that weight.

Marco stopped, panting. An incredible calm descended
for a few instants.

'We must go and get help,' I said.

'You go, I'll stay here.'

'We must go together. I won't move if you don't come
with me.'

'Where is your phone?'

'In my pocket, but it doesn't work.'

'It can give us some light, though.'

There was nothing of her on the surface, anyway. Marco
was persuaded that we couldn't manage by ourselves, and we
went out again.

'I've lost mummy's blanket,' he said, looking down at
himself.

'I know where it's, I'll get it.' A moment earlier I'd
stumbled on something soft by the window we had just
climbed out of.

I made sure I had Olivia's keys in my pocket and we
quickly headed for the car. Only then I felt the icy air and
the sounds of our mortally wounded world. The ambulance
sirens. Shouting, crying, calls for help, agitated voices in every
street. Helicopter blades whirling over the town. I feared
that that slight movement of air would crush it forever, with
us in it.

The figure of a man staggered before us in pyjamas and slippers, head between his tight fists. He turned for an instant and I glimpsed his eyes. I had seen him often on my visits to Olivia. We didn't exchange a word, perhaps he didn't even recognise Marco. Further on, two women were walking under the same shawl, supporting each other, avoiding the rubble at their feet, I heard them moan from time to time.

We stopped by the car. Inside, the familiar funny puppet hanging oblivious from the rear-view mirror. Only one of the sunshades had dropped, but there was something wrong with that anyway. The windscreen wipers struggled to clean glass covered in a sort of dry and dirty snow, expelled by the powdered walls.

The dawn of a pitiless day descended on us then, all at once.

We didn't know where to go and Marco, now a statue, no longer seemed to be in a hurry. I approached a fire engine and asked for urgent help in Via del Drago.

My mother reached us, I don't know how. She had managed to get through to me, after many attempts, and I had told her we were there, by Olivia's building. The rescuers wouldn't let us in, we could hear the sounds of the search and the voices upstairs. At times I deluded myself that my sister had answered them, at least, but it was always only the men talking amongst themselves to coordinate the operation.

We waited, at the prescribed distance, our eyes fixed on the door that had been opened and propped up. Marco, sitting on the ground, was rocking back and forth, wringing his hands. The skin on his knuckles went from purple to mortal white, instant by instant. Someone from the Civil Protection team had given him another blanket for his legs and feet, still bare. Later they offered us some hot tea, but we didn't feel like it. I don't know whom I asked for a cigarette – he didn't smoke and anyway, better not, he said, there could be some gas leaks. Towards eight o'clock a fireman came down with Marco's clothes and trainers; he put them on right away and started to walk a few metres up and down. His grandmother followed him with her eyes, her palms together and a slight tremor on her lips, perhaps a wordless prayer.

A little before ten the older man, the team leader, I think, came out. Apart from his eyes, protected by goggles, and the line of his mouth, his face was a mask of dust with an indecipherable expression. He removed his helmet from hair plastered with sweat and he stretched his arms. He got someone to bring out a chair for my mother. She must have understood, then. No more digging noises could be heard from upstairs. After a few minutes they brought out Olivia, already in a body bag. They laid her down in front of us, on a stretcher. She could no longer surprise us. We'd counted on that, until the very last moment.

18

When Roberto arrived they were already taking her away in the ambulance, with the siren off. They didn't even turn on the flashing light, there was no urgency. Only the stop lights turned red, down the road at the crossing. He must have seen them too, I pointed with my head in that direction the second time he asked after Olivia. None of us had answered the first time.

He put his arm around his son's shoulders and Marco let himself be hugged, passive and inert in his father's arms. Roberto was rattling on, slightly out of breath, about setting off right after the tremor, which had been felt even in Rome, that he'd been unable to get here sooner because of the road blocks.

'The two of us are going to the morgue,' I whispered in his ear, the one further away from the boy, nodding towards my mother crumpled on the chair in the middle of the road. Perhaps he hadn't recognised her yet, and in any case he did not dare approach her.

'Where is the morgue *now*?' Roberto asked under his breath.

'I don't know.'

'Where are you going then?'

I don't know where my voice came from to exchange those few words, I felt it pour like that of an alien from a detached and automatic place, an insignificant no man's land skirting the newly fallen bereavement. As for Marco, he had abandoned himself, unaware, to his father, surrendering in those few first moments the guidance of his scrawny lifeless body. Let's move this way, it's safer, Roberto was saying, and he'd submit, listless and docile, to the slight pressure of his hand. He even accepted a sweet the other put in his mouth, worried by the long time the boy had gone without food, but you could see that he just kept it under his tongue without sucking on it, as with a tasteless pebble that had ended up there by accident. I still can't figure out why my eyes noticed those insignificant details, while I helped my mother off the chair and steered her towards the car. A man dragging a suitcase with his head down stopped the wheels clicking on the cobblestone to give us way.

On the same evening of 6th April, Marco said goodbye to us; he was following Roberto to Rome. They came back for the state funeral: Olivia was one of the 205 coffins lined up on red felt, right next to the two stacked up together, a little girl's white coffin on the dark wood of her young mother's. Halfway through the ceremony I moved aside just in time to vomit, beneath the variable sky, the acid emptiness I had in my stomach. I wiped my mouth with the back of my hand and returned to my place next to my mother and Marco, in the first row, the one for the victims' relatives, bombarded by photographers and television crews. Roberto was right behind us; from time to time he would reach over to squeeze his son's arm.

Afterwards he left us alone and we spent a couple of hours together, the three of us, but we didn't know where to go. Not home – mine was inhabitable and so was the family home in the village – nor to the tent city that housed us: we had nothing to offer our boy. So we stayed in the car for a while and, when the silence became unbearable, I turned on the engine and drove around randomly. His grandmother insisted with her remaining strength for me to buy him a roll and a drink at a kiosk, and he tried to please her, he did, taking small bites he could not swallow. He gave up and folded the food into its paper bag, putting it down in the empty space on the bench where we were sitting.

'What do you do in Rome?' I asked.

'Nothing, I don't go out.'

'Your father told me he has enrolled you in a school in the neighbourhood.'

'Yes, he told me too.'

'When do you think you'll start?'

'I don't know, next week maybe.'

'Make sure you eat, please.' That was his grandmother.

Roberto phoned him and reached us a few minutes later. They had to head back.

At the camp there was a stagnant smell of meat cooking for dinner; I had to fight the urge to be sick. We declined the consultation with the psychologist, and laid down on our camp beds, by now incapable of bearing a standing position as well as our grief. Later a woman offered us a little soup, though even my mother wouldn't have any, not even out of politeness. I went with her to the chemical toilets and counted out her drops, then we kept vigil for Olivia one more night; around us people breathed heavily, shouted in their sleep, but she was not there. In the morning, we felt the lives of others awake one by one, we heard them yawn, stretching in the half-light, going over the cold, the nightmares, the military organisation of the camp, as if that were important. A stench of feet suddenly dissipated when their owner put on a pair of shoes that had lived too long. I noticed everything, and everything was distant, and nothing made sense.

We didn't know when we'd see Marco again. He'd answer our phone calls in silences and monosyllables: no, yes, dunno. But he'd be there and in no hurry to hang up. He'd exhale desolation into the handset, sometimes I would listen to his regular breathing for a few minutes, without saying anything. He didn't mention his father, and if I asked after Roberto he'd clam up. Things were already going wrong between them.

We were privileged refugees at the camp. Famous chefs would come and cook for our meagre appetites, and politicians would come and visit, suitably attired in casual clothes, their faces moulded in solidarity. Film crews would shoot them against the blue background of the tents while they pledged a new start for the entire affected area and praised the courage and dignity of the population so harshly tested. I'd go out for a walk to spare myself having to listen, or stay on my camp bed. In the evening there were shows and concerts for us, all free of charge. We weren't exactly in the mood, most of the audience came from elsewhere. Thanks to the earthquake, we had visitations from celebrities who'd never have thought of coming to L'Aquila otherwise, but nobody stayed the night. They'd go back to Rome, sheltered from the discomfort and continuing tremors.

No news of my workshop. I'd sent a friend to put a padlock on it, but he hadn't felt up to going in. Once in a while I'd remember the colours, and my wrist moving behind the brush.

After a few weeks I begged my mother to move to one of the hotels made available on the Adriatic coast, but she didn't want to know. She counted herself lucky to be at that camp, so close to the cemetery; she could reach it in a few minutes and spend all her time there, at the new tomb. I couldn't insist, I didn't want to leave town either.

The cold suddenly gave way to summer heat, without a half season. From early morning it was impossible to breathe in the tent. While we waited for the air conditioning to be installed we had to get out and think of something: where to go, what to do. The bed next to my mother became free, as the old man was going to Milan to stay with his son, so he told us when he said goodbye. We'd seen him phone his dead wife every day since 6th April. Not knowing how to use the phone memory, he'd dial the number on the big-button keypad, his old fingers careful to avoid mistakes. He clung to the hope that sooner or later she'd answer in person, instead of the recorded young woman's voice declaring her not available at the moment.

He was replaced by a man in his forties who looked a little unsavoury. He'd wake up early and disappear without a good morning, to come back after dark. There were rumours of strange dealings, people said he'd been kicked out of another camp. Only one night he kept quiet, every other he would masturbate with the grunts of a boar in heat. He'd take no notice of complaints, but one night he pulled a large clasp knife, and used it to carefully clean under his fingernails, in front of everyone. The Civil Protection contact officer promised to resolve the matter as soon as possible. Shortly before our neighbour was moved, my mother gave in and accepted the umpteenth invite from her sister who lived in Caserta.

From there, she called always at the same time, me first, then Marco. She would start by asking if *that pig* was still in our tent. I said yes for a couple of weeks, to let her have a rest from the camp. She said she was fine and that they were very kind to her, but I sensed in her voice the bitter taste of her relatives' bread. The last exhortation was food for me and fresh flowers for Olivia.

'Don't worry about Dad, I'll get him some as soon as I get back,' she'd say in earnest. Looking back, I find her floral discrimination amusing.

She cried when on the same call she heard that *that pig* was no longer there, and that we'd been assigned a unit in the C.A.S.E. Project. The next day she phoned at an unusual time; she was already at the station waiting for me.

19

Olivia calls from a long way away and I can't see her. Blinded by metallic flashes I cross a grey rock desert under an acid, perpendicular sun. The calling of my name seems to come from a set point along the soft line of the horizon. I walk towards it cutting through trembling waves of torrid air. I sweat drops of mercury, they roll down to the ground without soaking in. When I believe I am nearly there, 'Caterina' bounces from the opposite side, and the sound is repeated, exhausted, with a note of reproach for my late coming. I try to run, my strength sapped by the heat; the call allows me to get closer and then cruelly moves away, and then again, from echo to echo. I no longer know where to go; I go round and round, failing in my search. And the voice goes back in time, from adult she turns into a child, a new-born, the first cry, complete silence. She's born in reverse into a malignant and invisible womb, she dies a blinding death. I fall to my knees on the arid rocks and I wake up. From a room I cannot place inside the building, the usual dry and insistent cough welcomes me to reality.

My recurring nightmare since I found dreams again, many months after the earthquake. I never get used to it. It leaves my throat parched with guilt and impotence, a faint taste of blood. I drink from the bottle on the bedside table, next to the LED clock indicating a quarter to three. Olivia's vest, which I wear every night, feels just a little damp on my skin, it will slowly dry over the next few hours in bed. I stole two from her clothes and alternate between them. My mother doesn't know whose they are or pretends not to.

There isn't a sound from the room next door, where Marco is lost in the immense sleep of adolescence. I wait open-eyed to wake him at six; he's going on a school trip today. With a pang of anguish I imagine the bus driver, who I hope will have rested enough before getting behind the wheel, and will not stop at a bar while the kids are at the museum. Olivia would laugh at me and my fears, I can see her shaking her head, saying: you never change.

This nightly interlude, so dark, is always dedicated to her; while the sorrow of the other two sleeps I feel the loss cruelly. There is no need to hide. I could even cry, if the tears would come. I offer her my insomnia – someone must keep vigil for her, think over the unfathomable solitude where she is, where she is not. As per silent agreement, my mother takes the evening shift, and at times I hear her toss and turn between the sheets after completing her silent repertoire of prayers. She reaches for a handkerchief without looking, a brief sob escapes her. I don't know when her shift ends, and she doesn't know when I wake from the little sleep we share. In the background, her placated breathing whistles soft and rhythmic until dawn.

I spy on the phosphorescent minutes to pass the time; they change slowly then suddenly speed up around 3.32. Again, I squeeze my eyes shut for the duration of the tremor, again I taste the dust in my mouth. Every night Olivia tells us all over again what to do, tells me and Marco to go downstairs, she'll be right behind. Every night I try to undo what cannot be undone, playing out alternative endings in my mind. Usually I make the beam resist thanks to the seismic retrofit commissioned by my fantasy engineer, more cautious than the real one. Or it collapses an instant after Olivia has cleared it, with her son's trousers and shoes in her hand. Or a braver me stays behind to get those, while I send her out to save herself with Marco.

We could have swapped deaths, as we'd always swapped clothes, books, occasions. Her life would have been more useful; she would have brought up the boy. She would have helped him through his acne and the burden of becoming an adult. The acne cream lies abandoned on the bathroom shelf, where I put it, now near its sell-by date. He doesn't want it from me, or I don't know how to give it to him.

'When will I become an aunt?' Olivia had asked me abruptly, a few days before the earthquake.

'When I find a father.' Liar that I am, I gave her the stock excuse, convincing enough even for the aspiring grandmother. But I've never wanted children, never believed myself able to look after another, when standing on my own two feet is hard enough.

'True,' she added, thinking of Marco with a smile, 'And then they get to this ungrateful age and you nearly regret having made them, but it's worth it.'

She has bequeathed us this teenager, and I struggle with him. I put on a harsh front one moment, the next I feel guilty and give in under the weight of his sorrow. At the table he rarely looks at me, sitting in his mother's place. When our eyes meet I duck my head, ashamed to be there, alive by mistake in front of him.

It's time for him to get up. I close the door on the dog's muzzle and pause a little in his room, welcomed by the human scent. I never see him so close up. I observe his pale, uneven face in the lamplight. Some pimples have burst and the pus has become encrusted around the dawning beard. On the down of his upper lip minuscule drops shine like dew on grass. His forehead is sweaty too, at the root of his hair, before it curls. I get closer to the dry, parted lips; his mouth smells of deep, fasting mucous membranes. I softly touch his head in a sort of caress, he feels warm. I immediately pull my hand back, frightened by my gesture.

Bric saves the school trip by thumping the door with his paw, I open and let him wake his master. Later we take him to the bus, the others are already there, euphoric. Rash shows off a natural red crest on his freshly shaven head – I never would have imagined his scalp so freckly. He lifts a questioning chin towards Marco's backpack and he reassures him with a nod. Who knows what they're taking with them. Someone I don't know puts his arm around my nephew's neck and speaks fast into his ear, then they sneer at the girls, dolled up already at seven in the morning. By now all the luggage has been stored away in the belly of the bus, and the driver looks at his watch. They're waiting for the inevitable latecomer, who gets a standing ovation when he turns up.

Before getting into the bus, Marco picks up the dog in his arms and receives a lick which makes the boys laugh, then he transfers him to my arms, and says 'Bye, Aunt.' The others say goodbye to anxious mothers or sleepy-looking fathers. I look at the compact groups of parents without mingling, with a vicarious envy on his behalf. They're so different from our amputated family, they wear the smug look of satisfaction for their children's good school performance, and tragedies escaped.

Bric wants to get back to the ground and whimpers softly, a sort of creaking. Andrea's mum has kept aside too; we exchange a hint of a smile, she looks a bit run-down. I'd like to invite her for a coffee at the bar nearby but I give up, I wouldn't know what to say. I picked Marco up from Andrea's one afternoon last spring. They live in a M.A.P at Villa Sant'Angelo. The M.A.P. look like plastic huts, but there were pots of cyclamen outside and a neat lawn, a white cat busy with the first bluebottle of the season. Inside, the cumbersome presence of a father who doesn't even have a job since the earthquake. He never leaves those few square metres, Marco told me one day, when he was feeling talkative.

20

I felt relief yesterday morning, walking past his empty room. I was about to go in but my mother had beaten me to it, with an armful of bedsheets and determined to clean. As for me, I put two pairs of his trainers in the washing machine, and watched for a while as they went round banging on the side of the drum. Once she was done, I closed his bedroom's door. Bric laid himself down just outside and refused his food, in the end I gave up and opened the door for him. With the gait of someone who has been beaten with a stick, he reached the bedside mat and settled down to his suffering. I allowed him to stay the night there, so he could at least be comforted by the smell of his worshipped master's feet.

I don't miss him though. Now that he isn't here, I move with a lightness I had forgotten, as if gravity had been suspended. I have three days' holiday on the moon, while my nephew is on a trip to Florence and its surroundings. Even thoughts of Olivia cannot bring me down to earth, perhaps with a sense of guilt, however vague. There is nothing I can do for Marco, whatever he might get up to, whatever might happen to him. Someone else will have to deal with that, I am far away, taking a rest from the responsibility. The elastic band that circles my heart comes loose, and my heartbeat booms healthy in my chest. I return to being the girl I was in my previous life, occupied by herself alone. My mother doesn't need me, she has survived and prays to her God, following the daily grave-side rituals. I am free to myself.

I buy a pair of ballet pumps, brazen-red in anticipation of a spring that will not come. It's been four years since I wanted something new to wear. In my workshop I open the box and touch the leather, so soft and smooth, I take in its smell. I line up one step after the other, pleased with myself at the sight of the shoes. I sit down and kick my feet, like flaming flippers in the air. I put them back in the box next to each other, each pointing in opposite directions. I replace the lid and begin the wait for an opportunity to wear them.

He is not my child. Marco and I don't belong to each other. And if a twin had to die, I didn't want to be the one to survive. The earthquake lottery pulled a random number and split them up, Olivia and her creature. It saved me, and I am sometimes wistful for the end I was denied. I'm not a mother; he isn't the fruit of my narrow womb. He's someone else's, born of someone almost identical to me. I don't love him, I often do not love him, when I get home and smell his presence I feel an immediate discomfort in my stomach, and then I fall under the darts of his eyes. He scares me, as does the enormity of my task. I should be his spare mother. Instead, I am still a supply teacher at her first assignment, floundering in the face of her unruly class.

No help from Olivia. No sign from her final elsewhere. She remains apart, doesn't fling any words to the before-life of the remaining. We have lost contact, and she has lost her powers.

I find that hard to accept. Our menstrual cycles were in sync, as were some of our feelings. That's what it's like with twins. Since Olivia disappeared, not a drop of blood has dribbled from my uterus. All of her has died out along with her visible body. She won't talk to me, won't reveal herself, indifferent to the aloneness of those left behind.

Marco's father is scared of him, too. From time to time he takes an uncertain step towards him, ready to pull back at once in case of adverse reaction. He expects it, he starts off defeated, already unwanted. He phones him to ask to spend the day together, in Rome or L'Aquila, but his demure tone is a prophecy of rejection, which his son fulfils. I know that tone in Roberto's voice, like a whining cat. His lukewarm affection is adapted to surrender, to do without those he doesn't know how to reach. His interest in Marco is real and defeated, he falls back like troops weakened by a fear of never-fought battles.

But today I want to forget them all. I surprise my friend Silvia with an invitation, after she has tried a thousand times to flush me out. It's cold, just for a change, but I decide to wear the ballet pumps anyway, with my black trousers and heavy stockings. We meet in front of the Boss, and Silvia hugs me and laughs, moving my hair aside. We walk into the scent of ancient cellar: corks and wood soaked in Montepulciano wine, cured meats and white pizza, no longer the smell of cigarette smoke. For years now we've been going out on Piazzetta Regina Margherita to huddle, freezing, around our cigarettes. There aren't many people at this time in the afternoon, a few old-age pensioners playing cards and two women talking earnestly. Silvia is a regular, she stops a moment with one of the owners by the counter, the boiled eggs to serve with wine already on display. We sit in a corner and she looks at me again, shaking her head.

'I thought I'd lost you, by now,' she sighs, tracing the names carved into the tabletop with a penknife. 'I can't believe I'm seeing you here at the Boss again.'

'It has been a long time since I was here last,' I confirm, looking all around. 'At least in this place it's all just like before.'

'The day after the earthquake, I heard rumours the cellar had collapsed. I really thought then that it was the end for L'Aquila. But the Boss had survived. Thankfully.'

She suddenly stops, remembering Olivia's end. She feels tactless for what she's just said. I know how it is, I have learned to read, in the more or less carefree faces of those who haven't known loss, the awkwardness for the losses of others. I could say that I don't care much about the historic bar, instead I give her a forgiving smile and we move on.

After the usual glasses of red wine with crunchy *tarallucci*, they bring us *focaccia* and *frittata*, the inimitable Boss *frittata*, with coarsely-ground peppercorns inside it. I crush them between my teeth and savour them on my tongue, eating with the appetite I used to have when we'd come here after our classes at the Academy. University students start coming in, and in a few minutes the wine bar is full, the chatter and the temperature both rising. Silvia orders another two rolls, before they run out. In the middle of the room, someone called Danilo announces that, to celebrate his birthday, he'll do a henna tattoo for everyone present, on a body part of his choice. Busy chatting, we forget about him, until the young man comes to our table, surrounded by a curious and rather tipsy entourage. He gets too close for someone I don't know, he almost brushes me with his long, curved eyelashes.

'May I do a drawing on your left ankle?' he asks, while I pull back fearing his drunken breath. Instead he smells of orange and oriental spices. I stretch my foot to show him how difficult it would be to uncover the part that interests him. I offer him my wrist and he accepts, with a little reluctance. In a few minutes he has drawn two snakes entwined over a heart.

'Isn't that the symbol for a pharmacy?' Silvia objects.

'No, it's for sin,' he answers, and seals the drawing with a sort of transparent film. He kisses my hand and moves on to the back of my friend's neck, a rose for her.

The tavern closes early, everybody knows, but always goes into lock-in, at least until the Boss decides that enough is enough and opens the door, wishing everyone goodnight. This is a special night, Danilo must finish his round. It's nearly eleven when the town's air bathes our overheated faces.

After that, Silvia and I stroll along the *corso* towards Piazza Duomo, laughing at every opportunity. My telephone's imperious ring doesn't surprise me. Who could it be, so late, Silvia worries.

'Are you seeing anyone?' she asks hopefully.

I shake my head no and answer – the unknown number promises nothing good. It's one of the teachers escorting the school trip to Florence, he's panting a little, as if walking uphill. Marco has got drunk, he has been vomiting and trembling for some time, they don't know whether they should call the out-of-hours doctor.

'They were drinking in their rooms after dinner, he and his friend,' he explains. With an accusing note in her voice, she adds that they brought the beers from home, quite a few cans. That backpack, so full. Who knows how they managed to get hold of all that alcohol, two underage boys with little money.

'What do you expect me to do now, from here?' I ask, resentfully.

'We wanted to know if the boy has some health issues, because of the way he's trembling ...'

'There are no health issues. It's always like that when he's sick, it scares him. Has he got a blanket round him?' They'll find him one now, and we'll speak later.

Silvia understands and makes light of it. 'We all got drunk at that age, I did several times.' I don't answer. She gives up after a brief attempt to lift my humour, suddenly plummeted. I leave her in a hurry, promising to meet again soon, though.

In the freezing car a small Marco comes back to me, down with gastroenteritis one day at their home. Olivia was supporting his pale forehead and he would vomit, then tremble. 'Aunt, I'm afraid I'm going to vomit my whole body,' he'd said during a lull, turning towards me, his cheeks lined with tears.

When I call back he has finally gone to sleep.

21

I return the letter from the school to my mother's dry hands. She puts it back in the envelope with some difficulty and, in the end, a slightly impatient gesture accompanied by a movement of the lips that I can't decipher, perhaps a repressed curse. But it can't be, not in her mouth. Employing all the scanty elasticity left in her vertebrae, she draws herself up into the authoritative posture she used to adopt when we were little and she was preparing to give us a lecture.

'If he carries on like this, he won't be able to get away with it, next time,' she starts, shaking her neat grey head.

'I'd already arranged some private tuition with a young graduate, but he's not easy to persuade, is Marco.'

'But he must, he can't fail the year. Some children go bad after failing at school.'

She has relaxed a little, rounding her shoulders just enough for someone her age. She suddenly stiffens again in the dim afternoon light in the kitchen. By now I'm normally able to guess what's for dinner by the smell rising from the covered saucepans on the cooker top, by the leaves draining in the sink. Today, no such preparations are underway. I sit, and she talks down to me from the top of her short stature.

'By the way, what is the meaning of *inappropriate behaviour in class particularly during the school trip*?' she reads off the quivering sheet that she is looking at again.

'I don't know, but kids tend go a little wild on school trips.' I make light of it, as Silvia did with me the other night.

'Call your brother-in-law, call him right now – if he has rehearsals later he won't answer. He must behave like a father. The father of a boy who has lost his mother'.

Her voice breaks in her throat like a glass that has been cracked a long time. She swallows, bites her lip, and in an instant she regains control of herself and starts again.

'And he can't lose him too. Marco needs that one. You do too much already; you can't carry the whole burden.'

'You're here too,' I say, giving her a trusting look.

'I'm the grandmother. I love my only grandchild with all my heart.' Again she stops for a moment, pushing back against the tears.

'I don't want to tell him off. His father must take his responsibilities. Raise his voice, when it's necessary, say no sometimes.'

She carefully avoids calling him by his name, the son-in-law. Into this denial, she concentrates her persisting resentment towards him. 'If he'd stayed, she wouldn't have come back here to die,' drones the same old funereal chorus whenever my mother refers to Roberto, without ever uttering his name.

'I'll try to speak to him, it isn't the first time. I asked him over, remember?'

'Now you have something from the school too. He can't pretend nothing has happened.'

'He might worry, but I don't know what he'll be able to do with Marco. Roberto is too taken with his music.'

Perhaps I said it in an obliging way; she immediately flares up.

'There, I knew it! You forgive him everything because *he's* an *artist!*'

Her face goes purple, she's furious. Her voice alone rises from the chorus, dominating it.

'If her husband hadn't left her, your sister wouldn't have come back to die in the earthquake, remember that!'

'Mum, Roberto didn't ask for the earthquake. We won't be able to help Marco get closer to his father if you don't accept this,' I try to soothe.

'So now it's because of me that Marco isn't close to his father, not because of that spineless man! You always make excuses for him, you justify him every time, *he's a musician!*' she gives off, pitching her last word between solemn and sarcastic.

'Believe that if you want. In any case, I'll ask him to invite Marco to Rome for a few days.'

Her rage suddenly deflates, yielding to a dismay that invades her twisted face. In a few instants she's gone white, I worry about her balance and stand up ready to catch her.

'But what about school ...' she protests softly.

'There'll be a long weekend in a few days, I'll ask Roberto to take advantage of that.'

'And if he's away performing?'

'They can sort something out ... The problem is whether Marco will agree.'

The doorbell rings while my mother's staring at me open-mouthed, searching for something to say. The neighbour in perpetual mourning comes in, a shopping bag swinging at her side. Appearing reasonably familiar with her surroundings, she slowly unpacks some bags of flour and sets them out on the table. Wholemeal, I read, spelt, gram flour. Suddenly she feels the tension in the air, and looks at us, lost, the older friend first, then me. She retreats into her little body and whispers an apology, it isn't a good time, she says, walking backwards towards the door. But we've already composed ourselves, my mother is ready to fold her into her affection.

'Don't worry, Lorenza, you're not disturbing us. We're just putting some water on for tea. You've found the flours, I see ...' and her face opens up in a smile.

'Yes, I was thinking that tomorrow, when we get back from …'

'Of course, we can make some *fettuccine* or *pappardelle*. Shall we try the gram flour?'

'I don't know, I bought it, but I don't know it.'

'You can use that for *fracchiata*, it's a sort of polenta served with dry peppers fried in lots of olive oil and garlic. It's a dish of the Teramo area, I learned to make it from an aunt who used to live in Arsita.'

'My husband might eat that.'

'You too, a little,' my mother encourages her.

'It sounds a bit too rich for me.' The idea of food pulls Lorenza's mouth into a childish grimace of revulsion.

'You'd think that, but it's easy to digest, like polenta. You only need a little, just a few mouthfuls.'

As they talk in the kitchen, her black trousers appear emptier than ever, the belt wrapped around a void. Under her top, the breasts that in another life had given nourishment have shrunk into her ribs. My mother senses that I've been excluded from their sorrowful complicity; she turns to me and explains.

'Lorenza and I go to the cemetery together now, in her car. When we get back at lunchtime sometimes she stops here and we cook, then she takes the food home with her. Her husband gets in from work after two in the afternoon. We keep each other company.'

'Some days I can't manage by myself …' the guilty voice confesses. Then we drink tea, in silence, lost in thought. The biscuits remain untouched.

'I'll wait for you downstairs at nine tomorrow morning,' Lorenza takes leave. And now I'll phone Roberto, before Marco returns.

22

Lorenza is the last in a long line of shepherds with their roots in Castel del Monte, over 1,300 metres above sea level. Her great-grandfather taught himself to read and write, ordering books that took weeks to arrive, with the postal service of the time being as fast as a snail. He'd wait for them with the vigilant patience of someone used to following the flock on the golden expanses of Campo Imperatore. Back in the village at night, having secured his capital in the pen, he'd ask his wife if a parcel had arrived that day.

Trees were rare up on the pastures and for two months the sun would scorch the land bristling with grasses, but he wouldn't even bother to find a comfortable place to sit in the shade of a rock. He would read on his feet, walking slowly or standing still, a hand resting on the hazelnut stick, his hat casting a rounded shadow on the open pages. After consuming many volumes with the smell of sheep's urine under his nose, or in the dim smoky light of his house in the village, he started writing in small, black-covered exercise books. They were rhyming verses, accounts of exhausting relocations of stock along the pathways of the Apulian Tableland. Or diaries of him alone with the animals on the furry uplands, like fleas on the edible back of an immense mythological beast. He could also carve wood, and Lorenza still has a stool and some kitchen utensils carved by great-grandfather Francesco's gouge. She shows them to me when I take her the steaming *fracchiata* my mother has prepared without her help.

'Thank you, I had a temperature and didn't go out,' she explains, burning herself on the foil-covered plate. She puts it down absent-mindedly, without even a quick look under the foil. You can tell she has no intention of trying it.

'It won't be as tasty if it gets cold,' I tell her, pointing at the polenta.

'I'll reheat in the oven later, and try it then,' she reassures me.

From the vivid image of the shepherd poet she moves on to the grandfather, then her father and uncles, more ordinary people who were able nevertheless to hang on to their livestock through generations of men and sheep, down to the present day. Their flock still grazes up on the plane, in summer, now overseen by a Macedonian employed by the family. But the sheep now winter in large barns, feeding on hay while they wait for the ice to melt.

'My dad has withdrawn a little, since ....' Lorenza whispers. She never mentions the earthquake. If she gets too close, she jumps right back, into a randomly organised tale. She's talking about her mother, now, she was the one to give her a modern name instead of naming her after a grandmother, so as not to show her up in the world. She never left the village, her mother didn't, but she wanted her daughter to go, at least as far as L'Aquila. She died young, just in time to see Lorenza enrolled into a technical school in the district capital, and arrange for the Sisters of the Holy Family to host the girl at their boarding school during term-time.

The phone rings and she answers with distracted grace. Yes, she's better, she took an aspirin. No, not quite on a full stomach, but they'd had breakfast together, doesn't he remember? Tea and biscuits, more than one, really. She doesn't feel like eating now, she'd rather wait for him, it won't be long. There'll be a surprise for lunch. No, not her, the kind neighbours, that's how she refers to us.

She hangs up and apologises to me. I should be dealing with Marco now, he'll have finished eating with his grandmother; I must speak to him before he goes out. I look at the livid circles under Lorenza's eyes and then at the door, but she's started again, a monotone lullaby, a fairy tale without a happy ending. She tells of her only love, often pointing with her chin to the phone still warm from his voice, as if to evoke him. She remembers him frozen stiff under her window at the boarding house, in her last year at school, waiting for a whispered goodnight from above. In Castel del Monte, on Sunday afternoons, searching for her when she was out with her girlfriends from the village. And on Monday morning at seven o'clock, the model student would be on the bus back to L'Aquila for the week, only to get off at Ofena to get in his old Fiat 500, the windows fogged with his passion.

Always late for school, on Monday mornings, she'd slip in behind her desk among the giggles of schoolgirls jealous of her flushed cheeks and ruffled hair, of her lips swollen with kisses. They got into real trouble in the end. Lorenza, feeding the mother superior a dying grandmother story, pretended to bring forward her return home by one day, on the Friday instead of the Saturday. And so Antonio took her to his boyish bedroom late that night, without anyone in his family realising. They loved each other in darkness and silence, perhaps shutting one mouth with the other, and left the house at dawn, before anybody had got up. In a bar somewhere they had milk and brioche, the sweetest of their life.

They tried again a few times, until they got caught. One day she found her father waiting for her next to the mother superior, after lessons. They didn't speak. Instead of washing her hands and sitting down at the refectory table, she went to her room to pack her books, clothes and her mother's photograph. By the time she came down with her suitcase, the nun with the haughty frown had gone and her father had once more donned his hat over his good suit and worst intentions.

She remained shut at home for over a month, even the phone had been disconnected. Letters bearing the school logo would arrive, and be ripped up unopened. The grandmother Lorenza had passed off for dying would stay with her all day, in part to follow her son's orders and in part to comfort her. His orders were no visits, no post in or out, she wasn't even allowed anywhere near the windows. But on this grandmother Assunta had been quite flexible, when they were alone. And that was how Lorenza got to see a bit of sky, the stones of the wall across the road, and a corner of the square at the end of the street, criss-crossed by Antonio's pale blue Fiat 500 when he came up from L'Aquila. With a lover's intuition, she'd sense the boy's arrival in the village, and begin her watch. Once, he passed too close to the house, coming up on foot on the path, and she blew him a kiss beyond the glass then shooed him off with her hand, as her father was due back soon.

'It sounds like a story from another time, doesn't it?' Lorenza asks, and I nod so as not to interrupt her. In the meantime, she'd hardly been eating, then as now, and she'd lost weight, much to her grandmother's concern and the apparent indifference of the stubborn mountaineer who left at dawn and came back with the darkness. He wouldn't sit at the table either, he'd eat the little bread and cheese he'd taken with him in the morning in the misshapen pocket of his woollen jacket.

One afternoon, her Italian teacher arrived from the district capital and Assunta let her in. She even despatched a neighbour to fetch her son from the pasture, but it was hours before he made it back, more or less like any other evening. In the meantime, the three women had been waiting in the kitchen, the older woman keeping in the background at her chores, to give the other two the chance to speak freely. When her father returned without so much as a greeting, Lorenza disappeared into her bedroom. She didn't even try to listen at the door, and raised voices only reached her a couple of times. She covered her ears with her hands and could only hear her own heartbeat, fast under her fingers.

She was back in school within a few days, but she had to travel up and down on the bus every day, no more boarding house. All arrangements concerning her were passed on through her grandmother, her father still wouldn't talk to her. He hadn't been swayed by the teacher's threat to call the police, but by the not-so-veiled reference to the good soul of his wife, who would've been ashamed of him denying their daughter the opportunity to get her diploma.

They married young, Lorenza and Antonio, on 7th of August, feast day of San Donato the martyr, patron saint of the village and of epileptics. The echo from the fireworks boomed across the mountains, birds flew away from the bell tower. After the ceremony, Lorenza ran for a moment to the cemetery to plant a kiss on her mother's smiling picture, dragging her bridegroom by the hand, her white tulle veil wafting among the sun-drenched tombstones. A series of mutual acts of forgiveness had returned the growing family to peace a long time before.

For years, they had yearned for a baby. Antonio comes back before the story is finished and I sigh with relief. He greets us, then with both hands he gently caresses her face, as if to make sure she's still there, after the few hours they have spent apart. I leave them.

116

23

The owner of the villa is coming back tomorrow or the day after, he said so the last time he was down here, when he left the keys in my workshop so I can air the rooms upstairs once in a while. I've never been upstairs, I listen to the two loud clicks from the lock with my mouth open, like a little girl about to enter an enchanted castle. As I cross the threshold the complex scent of the house meets me, the ancient wood of the furniture and window-frames, the latest coat of milk-white emulsion on the plaster, and from the kitchen old spices and the memory of long-past cooking sessions. I start to move from the semi-darkness in the hall through the variable light of the rooms, respectfully skirting the fret motif on the grit-tiled floors.

Step after step, the ties of everyday worries become looser, with the occasional backwards tug towards the end. I find nothing to reproach myself for. I spoke to Roberto and then with Marco earlier, about the long weekend ahead – the 'bridge' between two public holidays which, it has now been decided, they will spend together.

'Bridge, what bridge? Over the Messina Strait? They're not building that any more,' my nephew the comedian commented at first, before saying no. But when his father called he must've caught him at a good time, unusually accommodating. It happens, with Marco, that the block of his rage will crumble in an instant when he comes into contact with his father. It can't be easy for him to face him, such a rubbery parent – he'd rather avoid him.

Still, he'll be on the bus to Rome by now. To make sure he didn't change his mind, I told him that his grandmother and I were off to Caserta, to visit Aunt Bice who isn't well. My blood, though, knew that Aunt Bice is fit as a fiddle and that we're not going to budge from here, and it flooded my cheeks in an instant with a thousand pinpricks.

I blush when I lie, I have done so since I was a little girl. I've never learned to control myself. My mother would notice in an instant the difference in hue between our twin complexions and find us out, even if it was always up to Olivia to tell the lies, while I'd be standing there with my head down. Thankfully Marco hardly ever looks me in the face and he only muttered 'Of course!' as if we went away all the time. Then he asked about Bric but I had the lie ready, I said that Lorenza would look after him, in her flat.

'Give her some dog biscuits, or she'll starve him,' he suggested, but with a sort of tenderness to his voice, unlike his usual display of cynicism. And it was about her, not the dog.

I open the windows and the panes tremble, the thin glass an accessory to draughts and dust; a lot of it must have filtered through over the last few windy days. Now it's flying around on the air currents forming invisibly as I walk. I immediately recognise the professor's room, the only one to betray traces of recent human habitation. Everything is in order, apart from an open book left face down on the bedside table, when he got sleepy while reading. Perhaps he'd been marking it with the pencil that has rolled to the edge of a surface occupied mainly by two piles of large history volumes. It's the subject he teaches at university, I believe.

Subjects, that's it, I feel better about that too. That young man fresh from his degree will help Marco make up for lost ground and improve the low grades in the last school report.

'Your brother-in-law will pay for the lessons,' said my mother emphatically.

'That's fine by me,' I replied. 'You're the one who didn't want to take his money for Marco's support, at the beginning.'

'But I've changed my mind about that now, you tell him that. And we can't manage anyway, with my state pension and your ceramics. He must pay for that.'

I smiled at the meaning hidden in her conclusion, that stretches beyond the physics and maths tuition. She stared at me, a little lost, like when she doesn't understand.

Daylight lingers on the hand-knitted woollen blanket, dimmed by the thick curtains. I can't resist, I start looking inside the landlord's wardrobe. A few jackets on coat-hangers, casual but smart, several white shirts, some checked ones. I wonder about the man's age, he must be around fifty. I shamelessly open a couple of drawers. Cashmere jumpers folded and stacked together, plain or braided, the ones he always wears. They softly give way under the weight of my hand on the chest of the first, a grey one.

The bathroom smells of stagnant water and soap, I find his perfume on the shelf, vetiver. I dab a drop on the blue veins of one of my wrists and rub it on the other. Warmed by the heat of my body, the fragrance evaporates up to my dilated nostrils, and keeps diffusing every time I move. In a cupboard under the stairs I bump into a vacuum cleaner; I take it to the bedroom and start to vacuum back and forth, humming along to the monotone bass. With my face to the window and my back to the door, I suddenly feel I am being watched. I jerk around and he's there, facing my silent cry, leaning on the door jamb with his arm stretched upwards, just as if he were at home. He looks on, wry and a little roguish, as my face drains of blood and the gadget buzzes away unperturbed, even when still. I'd like to suck myself up in shame, from my feet up, before I turn it off.

'I must have scared you,' he guesses. 'What are you doing with that thing? It isn't your job to clean. You know a woman comes from the village once a fortnight, it isn't as if it gets dirty when I'm away.'

'Well, yes,' I stutter. 'It's that ... yes, I know about Signora Argentina, but it's been windy so ... dust comes through the windows even when they're shut. I came upstairs to air the rooms, so I thought I'd just vacuum a little, that's all.'

'It's really kind of you but you shouldn't have bothered. Here, give it to me, I'll put it away.'

'No, no, I'll do it,' I nearly beg him, terrified at the thought that he might smell his own perfume emanating from me at every beat of my frenzied wrists. As I'm saying that I try to wipe them, unseen, against my trousers, in an effort to erase the vetiver. But perhaps he's so used to the fragrance he normally uses that he can no longer smell it. With an excuse, I escape downstairs.

Late in the morning he comes down and knocks, softly. I open only a little, I don't want him to see much of me. He surprises me by suggesting dinner and I immediately resolve to turn him down.

'But when ... and where?' my voice asks instead, without my permission.

'Tonight, upstairs. You can come up as soon as you finish work.'

'Well, no, I'll go home to change, I'm covered in paint,' and I open the door a little wider to show him the multicoloured stains all over me. He watches slowly, moving his eyes upwards until they meet mine, and there he stops.

'I don't mind you like that, but if you'd rather change ... Are you vegetarian?'

'No, I don't eat much but I eat everything. Just not much.'

'You look worried. You can trust me, I'm not bad in the kitchen.'

'Oh, I know that, it always smells nice when you cook, even from here. I have some pieces in the kiln, I'm a bit stressed about them, not dinner.'

'What are you working on?'

A series of bricks for a nature reserve. I finally move aside, and he comes in. I show him the finished ones, with the wild roses of Abruzzo. He didn't know there were so many, he likes the names, and reads them off one by one, below the drawings, and I listen to him utter in a low, deep tone: *rosa tormentosa, rosa corimbifera, rosa spinosissima*. I tell him about each one, there are many even around here. *Rosa rubrifolia, rosa sempervirens, rosa caesia*. Of course I can show him in nature, once they've flowered. *Rosa dumalis*. We'll find them all, if he feels like walking. *Rosa viscosa*. With my teeth I punish the lip that goes too far and talks too much.

'You know all there is to know about roses,' he observes, looking at the last one.

'Only the wild ones. I couldn't paint them if I didn't.'

His glance washes over me again. 'And this one, what is this?'

'Oh, nothing. That ... is an experiment, an attempt at sculpture.'

He touches the poorly defined shape, almost caressing the squiggly impressions of my fingertips.

'I'll wait for you later then.'

24

After my shower I open the left-hand door of my white veneer wardrobe, where I store my clothes from before, the ones I no longer wear. I never look at them, but I know they're there, hanging softly, devoid of substance. Their light weight stretches them downwards from the bony-shouldered hangers, deforming them slowly as they lose the memory of the one who once wore them. Someone bothered to recover them and return them with the rest of my stuff, after 6th April. I didn't care, then, I accepted them out of residual good manners, or perhaps so I wouldn't have to explain my refusal. I put them down somewhere, in a limp pile, and only cleaned them and hung them up here several months later. My mother wanted to store some of Olivia's clothes next to them, enveloped in the transparent covers from the dry cleaner's. I browse through them, mine and hers, as through the album of a life now foreign. She used to wear the flashy one at Roberto's concerts, when they were still together. The two black ones are identical, we bought them in Rome, not that many years ago. Labels removed, we left the shop laughing, looking like the twins we were. I'll choose this one for tonight, but not my one. It doesn't matter that I am thinner than I used to be, than she was, it's a one-size. Her clothes used to bring me luck, if I was going out with a boy for the first time.

I can match a jacket with the new ballet pumps. I find it difficult to locate until a corner of red cloth peeps out from behind a winter coat. I apply a trembling eyeliner to my eyes and hurry to surprise my mother at Lorenza's. I find them busy sewing and, after a puzzled examination, needles suspended in mid-air, in unison the two women wish me a good evening, almost alarmed by my unusual appearance.

'I'm going to dinner at a girlfriend's,' I enlighten them, even though they hadn't asked. In the rear-view mirror of the car I apply strawberry-flavoured lip balm which, with the line over my eyes, is all the make-up I need.

The professor has set the table with two plain amaranth-red table mats, with napkins in a lighter matching tone. In the low, warm light of the chandelier I recognise my plates, the ones with the flower pattern and blue line around the border. He bought them some time ago, I thought they were for a present. Still standing, at opposite sides of the table, we exchange a conspiratorial glance over them. A few candles float in a large bowl between the two place settings, spreading oriental scents, their flames reflecting in the wine glasses at either side. He fills these halfway and, while he helps the Montepulciano d'Abruzzo breathe with circular movements that I awkwardly copy, he asks me point-blank, 'How do you see your glass, half-empty or half-full?'

I sip to give myself airs. On my empty stomach, it'll go straight to my head. I didn't eat anything at lunch, so that I could be at least a little hungry in time for dinner. I answer, faking a confidence that isn't mine, anticipating its effect.

'Normally half-empty, but I could make an exception tonight.'

He almost laughs and strolls to the stove. While he's facing away from me, my internal judge pops back on duty for a moment to spit out the sentence: shameless. My host invites me to sit down and serves a dark, smoking stew.

'What is it?' I ask, sniffing.

'Goulash. I hope you don't mind paprika.'

'Oh, no, I like spicy food. I mean, I used to like it, when I ate more.'

'I can see you don't eat much. That's why I thought I would cook some meat, you look as if you need it.'

I touch my fork to one piece, uncertain for just one moment, then push it in while we wish each other *bon appetit*. At the first bite all my taste-buds stand to attention, and my tongue starts salivating, relishing the contact with the spicy food. For a few minutes I abandon myself to the ancient pleasure of food, forgetting the agent of this miracle. In the end I meticulously mop up my plate with bread and leave it the way I'd sold it to him. Only now do I raise my eyes and meet his, pleased, amused, shiny. He hasn't finished yet; he's been watching me.

'That was excellent, really it was. Tender and tasty. Where did you learn to cook like this?'

'It's my Hungarian friend's goulash. Would you like a little bit more, with some potatoes?'

'Ok. This is San Gregorio's bread, isn't it?'

'Yes, I really miss it when I'm in Bologna. Every time I go back I buy a loaf to take with me. That one is for tomorrow, I am leaving early.'

'Ah, tomorrow, already ...' I let slip, and a candle goes out just as I fix my eyes on it. He lights it again with a match; he had seen the wisp of smoke rise from the wick.

'That's why I insisted on having you round for dinner tonight, it was the only possible night.' He pours more wine in the glasses.

'You shouldn't have, if you have to get up early in the morning ...' A slightly whining tone escapes me.

'It's to thank you for cleaning my bedroom,' he jokes.

'I didn't even finish ...'

'Of course not, I interrupted you!' His tone becomes more familiar and he touches my wine glass with his, encouraging me to drink. I look at him to read in his face the traces of this shift in familiarity, and his greenish irises make me feel as if I've gone over a bump. He brings a mixed salad to the table. He has changed the CD, I recognise Miles Davis' 'Round About Midnight.

'It is nearly midnight,' I point out to him, indicating the music in the air. 'You should go to sleep. Tomorrow will be here soon.'

'I only need a few hours,' he cuts me short. 'Do you like jazz?'

'I had a boyfriend years ago who was mad about jazz. He'd take me to concerts everywhere, and we'd spend hours lying on his bed listening to old vinyls. These days I only enjoy him,' and point to Miles on the stereo, '… Coltrane, Charlie Haden.'

'Not bad for someone of your generation. I, on the other hand, had a girlfriend who was mad about opera and that completely put me off. Opera, I mean,' he clarifies in response to my questioning look.

'And the girlfriend?' asks the wine in my bloodstream.

'I got rid of her a long time ago,' he answers, satisfied. We stand up together. I collect the plates and he serves the fruit. I lower my head when, coming and going in opposite directions, we brush against each other, in spite of the plentiful space available.

'I should have a *passito* wine to go with dessert.'

'No, not dessert as well …' I protest.

'It's only *ferratelle*, my grandmother used to prepare them with a special iron tool I still have. But Argentina, the vacuum-cleaner lady, brought these ones,' and he wags a long and elegant finger at me. I don't know how many I eat, spread with pumpkin jam. We cheerfully empty the jar. On the settee in front of the lit fireplace, later, all that's left for us to do is sip *ratafia* wine; this one is Argentina's too, she has infused it with wild cherries.

When he takes his jumper off, a perfumed wave, warm from his body, washes over me. He turns the sleeves of his white shirt up a little, the cotton collar is slightly frayed from the friction with his beard. The shirt must be one of those he keeps here, not a new one. We look at black-and-white photographs of his family, immortalised in the last millennium in their Sunday best, severe hairdos for the women. Our index fingers meet over the stately bosom of the *ferratelle*-making grandmother. I pause a little before pulling back.

'L'Aquila middle bourgeoisie of the 1900s,' the historian summarises.

'Mine is a modest family.' I tell him about us with no embarrassment, about Olivia and Marco, about how worried I am for this teenage nephew, orphaned by the earthquake.

'Do you ever think about yourself?' – a professor's trick question to one of his students. He does me the favour of not waiting for an answer, it's a question mark he wants to leave suspended in mid-air, lazily nibbling away, like a sated woodworm.

A chunk of burning wood drops into the fire, and sparks fly. I rest against the back of my seat, holding my breath while I search for the aching strength to take my leave. It must be two in the morning. I feel it in the languid weariness passing through my body, combining the effects of wine and sleep deprivation. There, two o'clock on his wrist next to me. I tell him, that I must go. This time he doesn't protest, he only asks if I can manage the car after a few glasses of wine, perhaps the road is wet too. It was raining earlier.

'I'll drive you otherwise,' he offers. There is no need, really. While he helps me with my jacket, his watch strap tangles with a mischievous lock of my hair. He disentangles it delicately, ever so slowly, then he takes my face between his hands, his thumbs caressing the two patches of thirsty skin at the side of my nose, back and forth. The soap on his fingers hasn't quite neutralised the onion and celery chopped for the goulash. He brushes my mouth with a quick, light kiss. He breathes in and then returns, lingering, once, twice, as if already wistful. His voice, lowered by emotion, drops to a whisper.

'Red looks good on you … See you soon. And be careful, will you?'

I raise myself on the tips of my ballet pumps and return the cherry aftertaste to his slightly parted lips. I don't want him to come downstairs with me, I run down the steps. Outside, the after-midnight cold fails to wipe the memory of his hands from the cheeks he touched.

25

I hardly realise I've arrived at the C.A.S.E. so late. As soon as I open the door, I am roused by a raft of wind and the loud voices of an argument in the car park under the platform next to ours. There are people looking out of windows lit for the occasion – they can't see anything but they're listening, in the middle of the night. It happens sometimes, the neighbours tell of petrol thefts from parked cars, of drug dealing. Last week someone from the platform in front told my mother about a drug addict getting stopped and searched. At platform two, we have better luck, the worst that's happened to us is the breakage of the discharge pipes from the flats, which run exposed above the parking spaces. One morning, someone found his car bonnet or panoramic roof covered in dish-water or diluted faeces, his own and his neighbours'. The C.A.S.E. are already falling apart. They were built in a hurry, at too dear a cost not to last. A panel coming off here, paint peeling off there, dampness rising sneakily and stubbornly along the walls. The ochre yellow of the shutters identifying our block endures, as does the blue of the one next to us, the green of the one down the road. The people endure, amid enforced sharing and hostilities. We're all tense, worn down by the persistence of uncertainty. Tired of waiting for Reconstruction. Some confess they want to stay on at Coppito Three for good, they've got used to this artificial suburbia, to the lack of services.

'Who cares that there are no shops?' an old man was arguing with his neighbour the other day. 'There's no money to spend anyway!'

'Well done,' retorted the retired trade unionist. 'When they assigned you this luxury hovel they were counting on you getting used to it and giving up insisting they rebuild the town.'

Under the platform next door, the argument becomes a fight. Some of the onlookers have already called the *carabinieri*, and here they come, tyres skidding on the tarmac. I walk into the flat softly so as not to wake my mother and sit in the kitchen for a while, reviewing the flavours of the evening, right to the last, the sweetest, the lips of another. We never told each other our names, but we know them from the rent agreement. His name is Sandro, I've also seen it on the post delivered to the villa. Now that I have tasted his kiss, I no longer think of him as the professor. He'll be back in a month or so, an unbearable wait just now. But I'm scared of him; the dinner, not yet digested, takes a turn in my stomach, squeezed by a sudden spasm at the thought of finding him in front of me. He's the first since the earthquake to make it over my safety boundary. He carelessly breaks through the opaque bubble of mourning that I have retreated into, my refuge from desire and its complications. On the morning of 6th April, four years ago, grief expanded and filled all available space, like a gas. It has become my atmosphere, the only air I breathe. I haven't been able to feel anything else, I haven't wavered. Falling in love was the least likely of my possible futures, pointless too, since I couldn't tell my sister.

Somewhere outside something falls, pushed by the wind. Olivia liked to be involved in my love stories, she enjoyed it, gave me advice. In her absence, not even the wind dares contradict the silence left behind.

As for kisses, I endured condolences at the funeral, weakly returned greetings of friends from before, met by chance, from time to time. Silvia's kisses outside Boss, and that was it. Intimate ones like this, I had forgotten them. The dog comes to muzzle my ankle; he seems to have come to terms with the disappointment of Marco not coming back. Nothing is going on, it's only a moment of weakness. Tomorrow I'll be fine again. Today, actually: midnight went by a long time ago.

My phone vibrates in the red pocket; I haven't taken my jacket off. I think of Sandro, just renounced, perhaps he's awake and still wants to say something to me. It's the central police station. *Carabinieri* downstairs, and the police on the phone now, too. The officer asks if I am me, and Marco my nephew. 'What's happened?' The boy is fine and is waiting for me, they'll explain when I get there.

'When I get where?' I ask, bewildered.

'To the station, madam, I told you. You must come and get him,' the voice explains, stern and patient.

'What about his father? He's in Rome with his father just now, I don't understand … Have you phoned his father?'

A brief pause on the other side, perhaps the time needed to regain control and suppress a few choice words.

'Madam, your nephew is not in Rome with his father. He has been revelling with his friends in the town centre, the Red Zone to be precise. Yours is the only number he gave us, he says he lives with you and his grandmother.'

'I'll be there in fifteen,' I assure him.

My mother has got up, she appears pale and silent at the bedroom door. Instinctively I pretend, without looking at her, that I'm going to A&E for Silvia, who's had a small accident after our dinner. She seems to believe me and goes back to bed.

'Roberto, wake up and listen. You have to get on your way right now and come to the central police station in L'Aquila. They're detaining your son. I'll wait there with him.' So I harass him in the depth of his pre-dawn sleep. It doesn't take him long to respond, on the phone we retrace Marco's movements, while I drive and Roberto gets dressed. The scoundrel told his father he'd get there tomorrow, this afternoon rather, and he told me and his grandmother that he was leaving yesterday. He treated himself to a day's freedom, like the young Lorenza, I remember, going to sleep at Antonio's that first time. Our champion, instead, has been putting a bit of life back into L'Aquila, apparently, with his band of rowdy mates.

On my way into the police station I cross two father-and-son pairs, one after the other. Their faces. They're already going home, these ones. Last time I saw them the school trip was getting started, when they were in a very different mood. A policeman tells me what happened, then he takes me to the room where one of his colleagues is watching the more or less drunken boys before they are entrusted back to their families. There are four of them left and they seem to ignore each other, but the collusion that links them hangs in the air along with the smell of their sweat.

I don't look at him right away and we don't say anything to each other. I sit down and wait, motionless. Marco doesn't understand and dares not ask. I feel his standing body vibrate at a distance, trembling almost. Another boy is collected by his dismayed parents, the mother in tears. The officer's cracking jokes, looking at his watch; he must have seen plenty of these scenes. From a distance, the first glimmer of daylight filters through the grey blind rolled halfway down, and blends into the cold indoor light.

They had organised a party at an inhabitable house. They were racing around on their scooters in the end, making a racket through the deserted streets of the historic centre, pushing barriers aside if they blocked their way. Marco, without a helmet or a licence, showed off stunts worthy of an expert biker, on a friend's vehicle. Intercepted by an army patrol squad, they refused to supply names and documents, but did offer to share the beers they had with them. The soldiers had to call the police. When they got to the police station, one of the boys spilled his guts. They just wanted to have a bit of fun, he said. I assume that Marco had planned to stay with Rash later, there he is with his flaming mane, clinging slackly to the back of a chair, his head drooping. My nephew would surely have woken just in time to catch the L'Aquila-Roma bus as agreed with his father, who phones just now.

'Wouldn't it be best to take him home for now?' he asks, already trying to appease.

'No, we'll wait for you,' and I hang up, without even asking where he is. Marco heard my plan, and he's looking at me now. I look back at him, patches of his face almost reflecting the ruthless neon light, the livid pimples standing out. Deep cracks mark his dehydrated lips, the mass of his hair seems diminished by heavy grime. One day seems to have made him thinner, changed. Something about him is alien to me, and suddenly adult, next to his usual childish restlessness that not even his inebriation, now waning, seems to have soothed. But he's controlling himself; he doesn't stride up and down the room, but stands in one spot, next to the radiator, and there he tries to give a shape to the irrepressible energy that agitates him. He pulls the cuticles from around his nails, one finger after the other, quickly but methodically. When he runs out of fingers, he works on a stain on the floor with the toe of his shoe. I don't think he drank that much, the wheelies on the bike must have intoxicated him more than the beers. The other two are snoring on the chairs. The guard observes them for a moment over his glasses, one first and then the other.

'Lions by night, pussies in the light,' he comments, talking to me. 'It's just a saying,' he clarifies, as if to apologise. Rash's father doesn't come in – his son is called out while he waits for him in the room where the paperwork is being sorted. Before staggering out, the boy glances at Marco, who helped the guard wake him up. Rash must have wanted to ask him if I've gone mad, what am I waiting for. Marco shrugs.

It becomes difficult for us now, with the last one gone, furiously shaken by an irate parent. We're alone, only the policeman in the background. The clock on the wall seems impeded by a contrary force that slows the rotation of the hands and compels them to linger on each minute. I remember the book I'm reading, in my handbag.

Maria Barbara gives a half to each twin. They study their pieces intently and, without a word, exchange them. She does not attempt to understand the meaning of this little ritual, knowing only that it does not spring simply from a childish whim. With their mouths full, the twins embarck on one of their long, mysterious confabulations in the secret language known in the family as Aeolian[1].

I read and reread this several times, I can't concentrate. I go back, to understand that the text refers to the two halves of an apple. Food, toys, shoes, Olivia and I were the same when we were children, before using them we would swap the things we were given, even if they were exactly the same.

'Any chance of getting out of here? We've definitely made fools of ourselves, I guess we can go now.' He speaks as he stares from the window at the metallic dawn spreading over the town.

1   From *Gemini*, by Michel Tournier (The Johns Hopkins University Press, 1997)

'Forget it. You're not going back to your grandmother, that's for sure. You're going with your father, the two of you can sort it out. As for making fools of ourselves, you've got quite a nerve to worry about that now.' I put the book back in my bag.

'You've got issues, you know that? Just in case you haven't figured that out,' he announces in a sombre tone.

'Maybe, and one of them is you.'

The vicious comment escapes me and I can't take it back. I have again been caught in a squabble with him, a contest over who can hit harder. He doesn't answer right away, he pretends to be interested in what little he can see outside, before turning to me.

'I'll relieve you of this problem soon,' he promises, or threatens. Then he swallows; under the thin skin of his neck his too-new, too-sharp Adam's apple rises and then immediately returns to its place, still, apart from a slight quiver.

We barricade ourselves in two stiff armours of silence. Even the guard is quiet, thumbing through some papers, perhaps his shifts for the next few weeks. Then he sticks a finger up his nose and starts working away, oblivious. Our presence has become so normal for him that he's forgotten about us. And Roberto isn't coming – they must have stretched the motorway this very night, just for him. He doesn't even have traffic as a mitigating factor, at this hour, and in any case there never is any on the way to L'Aquila. A long-held rage begins to rise in my chest, an urge to kill him, if he hasn't already perished in an accident. He arrives eventually, with the morning.

26

He had invited me and Olivia to dinner at his, after school. In the dim light of the hall, his mother welcomed us with two pairs of slipper pads: our shoes must not mark the waxed marble floor. Roberto stepped on his and moved with the ease of one who has long practice of sliding on felt pads without lifting his feet from the floor. The house was impeccably tidy; its mistress had enchanted the dust, forcing it to remain suspended in the air away from the smooth, dark surfaces of the precious wood furniture. Not to mention the grand piano, seemingly shielded by a glass case that only the young virtuoso's talent could possibly unlock. Olivia, though, didn't perceive the invisible barrier between us and the instrument. With a daring finger she pressed a key, and stole a note.

'Don't, please!' the lady instructed sharply, jumping up to lower the lid over the keys. She pierced her son with her eyes for the unforgiveable carelessness and went back to the kitchen. He didn't seem too bothered, a nonchalant gesture suggested we shouldn't take notice.

We sat at the table a little puzzled, Roberto observing us amused. We weren't quite sure how to use the cutlery correctly – at home in the village we had other things on our minds. The woman would come and go between the stove and the dining room, the two of us trying to eat quickly when she was out of the room; her glance made our mouths and hands unwieldy. While I was cutting my escalope, Olivia started to poke me with her elbow and had a fit of the giggles. Our companion stung her with a quip and she kicked him under cover of the tablecloth, sliding down the back of her chair. They weren't in love yet, or at least they didn't know they were.

I relaxed a little once I understood that Roberto's mother, only superficially aware of us, regarded everything from a secret distance. After dessert we stood up and I warily sniffed around. There was something missing in the almost aseptic perfection of those rooms. There was no man in the silver-framed photographs in the living room, or rather there was one but it must have been a grandfather, surely. For the rest, they were all photos of Roberto at various ages, with or without his mother, some pictures of her as a girl. One in particular attracted my attention. It would have been the photo of a happy family, with the parents' arms crossing behind the boy's head, each with a hand on his shoulder. But the white border only went around three sides, and on the left the paper had been carefully cut along a line to the side of Roberto's body. The scissors had amputated the father, all that was left of him was a piece of arm and four male fingers on the orange T-shirt of the six- or seven-year-old boy smiling at the camera with half-closed eyes and his nose crinkled at the splendour of the day.

'They are waiting for you in Roberto's room.' The woman made me jump, her tone icy. I reached the others under her commanding stare. Later, when we were about to leave, I glanced furtively at the photograph. It had disappeared, like the memory of the man who had once lived there.

The mystery of his disappearance continued through the years, including those of Roberto and Olivia's marriage. If anything, with the passing of time that reticence seemed to have infected her too, and if I occasionally tried to ask she would answer, irked and gloomy, that she didn't know anything for sure. Veiled, ambiguous references gathered here and there later persuaded me that it must have been a suicide or a flight without return, far from the family, and from the mistress who ruled it.

On the phone, Roberto had said that he was about to dress and would be in his car shortly, to reach L'Aquila within an hour or so. But now he smells of bubble bath and he's wearing carefully matching shirt and trousers, rather than clothes grabbed in a hurry out of a wardrobe. And on top of that, instead of slapping him, he's offering Marco a brioche and *cappuccino* collected from the bar down the road. He offers the warm beverage and, when he opens his mouth, I can smell the aroma of the coffee he has just consumed himself.

'You must be on an empty stomach, surely,' he says, attentively.

'The police station canteen doesn't open until later,' I cut in.

Marco is confused. He has taken the cup and paper bag as a reflex, but then he hands them back and remains there, arms in mid-air. He looks at me for an instant, without rage, as if to ask me what he should do. I shrug my shoulders briefly, showing my helplessness. They feel heavy and stiff. We haven't slept a single minute, neither of us. In the meantime Roberto is trying to offload the awkward breakfast he's been left with by offering it to the guard. He doesn't even try with me, I'm leaving already.

I find a green velour settee in front of the workshop. Sitting on it, a notebook page folded in half, kept in place by a small stone or it would've flown away by now.

I have to make space for some bookshelves, perhaps you could use this to have a rest from time to time. It's a family piece. There might be space for it amongst your paints. See you soon, Sandro.

I shiver every time I read it again, in particular the words *you could*, *your paints*, *see you*, all the bits that include *you*. They make me believe I exist, that someone might appreciate my little life. I put the sheet and improvised paperweight in my pocket, I leave my hand there, to warm them in my palm. And it's easy to lie down on the padded upholstery. I fit, if I bend my knees a little. Inside the ear resting snugly on the slightly worn armrest, my blood pulsates quietly, it reminds me of listening to sea-shells. The last image I remember is the veining of the few new leaves, on the lower branch of the maple tree, backlit by today's sun. I hadn't noticed the first few buds opening. All my aches fall asleep with me, one after the other.

I don't know how much later, the tyres of the Italian postal service utility car skid on the gravel in the drive. For a few instants I hold between my lashes the gobsmacked expression on Lucia's face, standing still with the post in her hand.

'Hello. Everything OK?' she enquires cautiously.

'It's fine, Lucia, thank you. I sat down for a moment and fell asleep. I'm fine.'

'It's just that normally sofas aren't kept outside. Anyway, you look very smart this morning.' The air barely stirs the hem of my dress. I struggle to sit up and look down at my red jacket and ballet pumps.

'It's a long story. I have to move this inside, the professor left it for me.'

'Come on, open up and I'll help you. It looks heavy and you are a waif.' I don't know how Sandro managed, by himself on the stairs. While we draw breath in the workshop, Lucia strokes the green material with a connoisseur's hand.

'They don't make them like this any more, solid and handsome. It'll last a lifetime.' She sighs and looks at her watch, she must get on with her round but she can't resist.

'What a man, that one, hey? Women swoon after him …'

'Really?'

'Why, didn't you know? Well, of course, you haven't been working here very long, and over the last few years he has calmed down a bit. But before ...'

'Before?'

'He'd bring a new woman every time he came down from Bologna, some beauties ... all very refined, mind you, simple dresses, low heels ... the sort that fall for intellectuals, you know?'

Like a killer blade, I see again what must have been a woman's scarf, hanging from the coat-rack upstairs, perhaps left behind by one who'd forgotten the cold outside. I didn't want to see it yesterday, I parked it at the periphery of my memory.

'Maybe they worked with him ...' I venture, my words trembling a little.

'Yeah, right, where have you been living? And even if they were, these guys take advantage, with the excuse of work they end up .... What have you done?' She's seen my face change, and guessed.

'Damn, you like him too. Couldn't I just shut up for once? Don't worry, come on ... he might have changed. It's been a long time since he brought anyone back, it's just that he's hardly ever here, he only comes once in a while for a rest.'

'No, not at all, I'm not interested, really,' I proclaim, trying not to give anything away.

'Better that way, then. And he's too old for you, anyway.'

She doesn't believe me, and hurries away to make up for lost time.

27

I sink my hands into the cold dampness of the white clay. It reacts to my squeezing by escaping resiliently through the spaces between my fingers. I work the mass to let it get used to my temperature, testing its willingness, it seems ready to submit to a form. It softly yields to pressure, allows itself to be reduced, lengthened, smoothed round. The palm presses its lines into it, life, heart and destiny, before they blend together and are lost in the movements that follow. Now the mass is as warm as my skin, and more docile still. I give it the rough shape of a woman, the legs only two truncated cones, the arms open to the air, stretching up, ending in a thumb on one side and the four fused fingers on the other, with no detail. She is leaning passionately forward, her triangular face turned to someone on her right. For her hair, I shape separate, slightly curly strands with the point of a loop tool, stretching them backwards to indicate the wind. She will remain all white, apart from her hair, and the flared dress on which I find myself sculpting a belly button.

I will paint vertical blue lines on the fabric. I start to outline the feet, but then decide to bury them in the stand on which I set her down. She is now a prisoner of the earth. With her little eyes, she looks at the mysterious interlocutor at her side and cannot reach him. I finish the thin face, the steep slopes of her nose. At the last moment, with a single stroke of a hardwood stick, I carve out the unending scream from a mouth I had left sealed until then. She's ready for the kiln now. I clean the tools that were a gift from my friend

Franco, a potter from Castelli, and put them back in their case. I nearly didn't take them, I'll never use them, I told him. They'll come in handy, sooner or later, he answered from inside his red beard.

It's Olivia's scream. I thought it was mine, but now that the woman is finished, she looks more like her. There is more than wind in that flying mane, it is the vital effect of her inner energy that reaches throughout the length of her hair and beyond, to the surrounding atmosphere. I recognise the dress. Even if she never had one like it, it could be hers, she'd like the blue stripes.

Perhaps she's cross with Marco, screaming at him to do what she knows to be impossible: to tidy his shoes and his unripe emotions. Or perhaps she's railing at Roberto, she wants to make him behave like a father. I have to wait until I wake up in the night to realise that she's screaming for me, I'm the one who has torn her clay mouth open. A rapid sequence of memories rips the darkness around her, and in an instant I learn to read in the past the signs that back then I didn't want to see.

Olivia would climb the apple tree faster than a cat, and straight away stretch an arm from above to help me up. She'd pull so hard that at times I'd lose contact with the bark and I'd find myself chewing on a fruit without knowing quite how I'd got there. I wouldn't notice the blood dripping from her knee, the sweaty fringe sticking to her forehead in little commas. She seemed to be able to do everything without effort, without pain. She didn't know how to complain, and this not knowing is how she lost herself in the end. Nobody, other than our mother, had ever really paid attention to her. I even denied her my jealousy, a misshapen form of attention. Olivia was simply the best part of me. I willingly showed her my weaknesses so that she could take care of every one

141

of her younger twin's fragilities, she who was so full of grace and fortune.

As happens to those who appear to be too strong, she wasn't protected, she seemed not to need it, independent and invulnerable creature that she was. Some people even feared her, ran away from her.

Giulio, for example, who used to come to the village in summer to spend the holidays with his grandparents. We'd always had fun together, but that time he had come back different, with an already adult Roman patter in his mouth and a desire to be alone with Olivia. She liked that city air of his, they'd go wandering on their bikes and stop off to explore places and each other's bodies, so new and awkward. One morning Giulio flew into the brambles of a ditch, scraping himself up a bit. He couldn't move for the shock of seeing his own blood, but she grabbed him under his arms and dragged him onto the road, where she stopped the first car coming by to ask for help. After that, he never looked for her again, and left as soon as possible.

In the silence after midnight, Olivia screams herself out, from that earthen throat. She opens the hidden album of her years with Roberto which, out of convenience, I chose to believe happy. Full of himself and his music, he didn't love her enough, he hardly even saw her at times. He forgot birthdays, never noticed when she was sick or exhausted. He would sometimes bring her a present when he came back from a concert, his suitcase full of success and clothes for the wash. On those occasions he found it easy to gratify her; with the echo of applause still filling his head he could be generous with her, for a few moments, before emptiness started again to eat at him from the inside.

Marco's birth didn't change him. He took on fewer commitments during the first year, he wanted to be there. In the half-light of some afternoons, he would keep his fingers and left ear on the piano, his eyes on the child a few steps away, silent as if aware he was being watched. The artist sought, in an almost painful tension, to wrench from the keyboard the secret correspondence between sound and the light in his son's eyes. For him he composed a few pieces in which the dark curls vibrated like little bells. Other than that, he'd loaf around distracted by a distant voice, barely audible yet persistent. He missed the orchestra, the public falling silent as the instruments were being tuned, before every beginning.

Olivia gave him back his freedom, returned him to the migrations of musicians. She told him she'd manage on her own. So their home returned to being Roberto's stopping station, his resting place. Sometimes he would return truly exhausted, so much so that even a few kilos of child proved too heavy. Stubbornly in love, she justified and understood.

Olivia brought Marco up in the joyous expectation of a truly special parent and if Roberto, on his return, tired of his son and pulled back, she'd catch his childish attention as in a game, to ensure he wouldn't feel in that new distance a surrender or, even worse, a rejection. For as long as she drew breath, my sister gave Marco an imaginary father.

She screams now, this inorganic woman, for herself and for the boy. She says she has been neglected, he has been neglected. That loss reproduces itself in future generations, like a hereditary fault, an accursed necessity. That's what happened to Roberto.

They were just teenagers when they met, and yet Olivia came too late for him. He carried within himself the damage of a final desertion combined with the rigid control of his mother, who had been left behind. The kiss of the princess did not transform him, he remained a toad. No one could have healed him, not even my omnipotent twin. Her posthumous scream complains for him too, the man who, unable to be saved, in the end betrayed her.

I saw them over the years, more so when they lived in L'Aquila. I've seen Olivia's mood become tinged with black, I've seen her lose her hair, one time. But she had so much of it, it wasn't even noticeable. I didn't speak, coward that I am, I didn't ask her how she was, and she was silent too. I couldn't do without my certainties about her. Tonight I discover that she wasn't always happy.

28

Marco came back from the capital with a last-generation mobile phone. Roberto wanted to drive him home and came up to the flat, just time for a coffee before going back. We all smiled at Bric fussing over his returning master, he even became emotional, the way dogs do. The dog too was made a fuss of, to make up for lost time, and became confused with joy. They disappeared to the bedroom, but the door was left open.

Perhaps called back by the small sound of the empty cup against its saucer, Marco came out of his room a few minutes later, to say goodbye to his father. He didn't pull away from the hand on his shoulder, and said 'Goodbye Dad', his eyes lowered. They seemed to have achieved a sort of familiarity, in these last few days. The expensive gift played its part too, I guess.

'By the way,' Roberto asked at the last minute, 'How is Aunt Bice, down in Caserta?'

I hesitated, thrown by the effect of my recent lie and by how easily Olivia's ex-husband still named acquired relatives as his own.

'Better, thank you. We have only been back a couple of hours,' my mother answered dryly, to cover for me.

I think I saw a girl on the screensaver of Marco's new phone, it must be that Irene who lives in the same building as Roberto. Long hair, large glasses as is the fashion these days, the perfect plump face of a just-ripe fruit. But it was only an instant; he felt my eyes on him and promptly dropped her in his pocket.

'Here, you can have this one, it works fine, and you can get rid of that thing,' he said, handing me his old mobile. 'I'll sort it out for you, you don't know how to do it,' he pontificated while swapping the SIM card. I understood little of the brief lesson on the most complicated functions. I won't use them anyway and he knows it.

The other novelty is that he has decided to take care of his acne: I have found the wrapping from a special soap on the washing machine in the bathroom, ripped apart with the usual grace, and, scattered on the shelf, the cream's packaging, the information leaflet he must have read, and the top of the little tube, which had naturally been left open, with a bubble of product hanging from it.

On alternate afternoons he goes to see the young man helping him with the subjects he needs to catch up on, and a couple of times I have even caught him with a book, in the evening at home. He was wrapping the entire length of his curls around his index finger, one after the other, with the expression of a sacrificial lamb or someone who has unwillingly surrendered to a shameful occupation.

I could be optimistic, but that was an unusual state of mind for me even before, let alone after the earthquake. I see disasters everywhere, in a future perhaps not too far away. I protect myself by always counting on the worst happening, so that it won't surprise me ever again. Marco's life tastes of ruins. At times I imagine him a drunkard, a drug addict, a hobo. For now, in the short term, a failure at school. If Olivia could've done so, she would have handed him to her twin like a difficult test to an unconfident student, hoping she would use her resources. And at every difficulty, I feel unworthy of a mother's trust.

At times I am dazzled by a bright opening – other plots become possible. That Roberto and Marco might find each other now, after their infrequent contact, that Marco might overcome his loss and the mistakes of the weak surviving adults. He did drink from those blue-veined breasts a rich and heavy milk for much longer than other children, a reserve of warmth and human nourishment that no tremor can ever take away from him. On 6th of April 2009, Olivia had already handed to her son strength and resilience. They still have to mature, despite the inability of us, the unsteady replacements, to lend certain and firm support. Marco will surpass us, he is the only heir to his mother's powers. In a dream I found the pitted skin of his face under his bed, as if he had shed it, leaving scars and spots attached to the old one. He will leave his adolescence behind him, as all children do. With a fairer outlook, I would already be able to see, against the light, the man he will become.

'Here, I brought you this from Rome,' he announces, handing me a small packet.

'And you've been hanging on to it until now?' I ask, taking it from him.

'Well, I'd forgotten …'

He leans his back against the wall and with the tip of his foot traces diagonal segments on the floor, one way and then the other. Slowly I pull away bits of adhesive tape with my nails, so as not to ruin the coloured paper underneath, which retains the slight dampness of his palm. Once I have also removed the bubble wrap, I am left with a glass bubble full of water, with the Colosseum under a minuscule snowstorm. When the last flake lands, I shake it again and enjoy the new storm. When I do it for the third time Marco clears his throat, embarrassed at my inane smile.

'So it's true that you like these bubbles.'

'Who told you?'

'My father, it was his idea to get you one.'

'Yes, it's true,' I confess to the upside-down face. 'They were always making fun of my collection, he and your mother. But they gave them to me, they'd bring me one back from every trip, every holiday.'

'Where are they now?'

'The bubbles? All broken, pretty much, they were in my old workshop, on a shelf.'

I shake the sphere again, and again it starts to snow between us. I breathe on the glass and wipe away the greasy finger marks with the sleeve of my sweatshirt.

'I've never known what the snow is made of, or even if the liquid is water or something else,' I confide in Marco.

'You should check, I think some might have survived.'

I shrug and we remain silent.

'They've started on several building sites in the centre,' he then says. I recognise from the change in his tone that he's throwing me a bait.

'I've seen that,' I answer tersely.

'When will they start with ours?'

'Ours ...?'

'Our homes. Yours and mine. When will Reconstruction start for us?' He enunciates the words one by one, as if talking to a deaf person.

'I don't know for sure. The bureaucracy is mind-blowing, it slows the process down, every time we're nearly there something else comes up. Work has started in the main streets of the town, but in the inner districts nothing's happening yet.'

'Bastards, as usual. But are you dealing with it?' he asks raising a questioning eyebrow.

'Of course I'm dealing with it. With mine and yours, and your grandparents' house in the village, too. You can

148

look in there, there's a mountain of applications, technical specifications, reports.' I point at the relevant cupboard.

'I don't care about the paperwork, but I want to know what's happening. You must tell me everything that's going to happen, from now on. It's my house.' He becomes agitated, and bangs an elbow against the wall.

'Of course,' I reassure him.

'How are they going to rebuild it?'

'They'll have to demolish it first.' I would have preferred not to have to tell him that.

'Do they really have to? Only part of it has collapsed. If they demolish it, how can we be sure they'll rebuild it as it was? I want it back as it was.' A shrill anxiety returns him for an instant to the voice he used to have a few years ago.

'You don't need to worry about that, there's a project in place. You will have your house back, with the same stones, the same bricks, but earthquake-proof, to be ready for the next one. We get one every 300 years.'

'Come with me on Sunday. Let's go there,' he asserts, confidently.

'Are you crazy? We can't, it's dangerous, you know that.'

'It isn't dangerous. I'll even give you a helmet, if you want. Trust me, for once.'

He has fallen asleep with the bedside lamp still on, and when I get up to get some water I can see the light through the door left ajar. I go in to turn it off. Marco turns under the covers, mumbling, and his phone falls to the floor, on the mat, thankfully. When I pick it up, a casual gesture is enough to shed light on the thoughts he has exchanged with his friend.

I read them with no great shame, without paying attention to her responses, telegraphic and a little frivolous.

Today I chased in the traffic a car just like the one my mother used to drive, I nearly got run over by a lorry. The head inside it was the same too seen from the back. It's not the first time she drives past, that woman, but I've never been able to see her face.

I realise that I'm waiting for her, my mother. If the door opens at home, I immediately think it's her coming back to surprise me, and instead it's my aunt.

I open my eyes in the morning and smell her presence in my room, like when she used to wake me up to go to school. I even feel her hand on my forehead, not always though. I don't know she's dead when I sleep, I remember when I wake up but not right away, after her perfume's gone. Then I remember where I am and who with.

29

Being considerate, Marco uses the key I pull out of my handbag, but I'm sure that in some way he has managed to open the padlock lots of times, since I changed it. I have followed him to Via del Drago in the fragile sun of the afternoon, without worrying about possible patrol squads – he knows how to avoid them. We've taken a precise route, certainly well tested, the barriers have already been moved aside just enough for someone as skinny as him, and me, to get through. Only at the opening of one alley he kindly made space for me and then left the gap as it was, made to measure for our return.

Before, in the centre, he simply lifted his eyes to indicate the building sites, the scaffolding over the buildings being restored. He was walking a few steps ahead when I said something he didn't hear because of the continuous vibrations from the pneumatic drills, the screeching of grinders cutting through metal. I wanted to comment that they're working only in the most visible streets of the town, as we were saying yesterday, but I didn't repeat that as we penetrated deeper into the Red Zone. He must have noticed by himself, that silence has fallen.

No doorway in L'Aquila is so easily yielding. Marco guesses my surprise and explains that he has shaved it at the bottom, where it was dragging against the floor. There's no more need to pretend now, and he discloses without restraint his regular visits to the inhabitable building. He wipes his feet on the mat and starts to climb the stairs, without precautions. I hesitate to follow him, frozen in the motion of taking the first step.

'Don't worry, it's fine. Do you want the helmet?' he asks, pointing to a yellow one hanging on a nail along with the painting it partially obscures.

He has turned back and speaks to me from above, with an almost tender tone in his question. I shake my head no, reach him on the landing and lean against the wall. My fingertips find the sinister break of a crack, and I pull my hand back. He precedes me in the living room he has divided in two, like his heart, I believe.

A half metre below the ceiling he has stretched a rope between the supporting beams at opposite sides of the room, to support a series of ethnic-print cloths which hang right down to the floor, forming a sort of screen as wide as the room. In this way he has cut off from sight the exact place where his mother died, where the beam felled her.

On this side, he has cleaned and rearranged everything. There's only a little bit of domestic dust, fine grained, the sort a sixteen-year-old boy doesn't even notice. He's pulled the table to the middle of the diminished room and pushed the sofa towards the dresser with the broken glass doors, only there's no longer any trace of the shattered pieces; the now empty door frames the unbroken things he has rescued. I recognise some cups from a set I had painted for Olivia. Behind them, a few crystal wine glasses, the ice bucket. He must've washed them, I don't know how, there's no water coming from the taps.

The furnishings seem to have come from some other home, where they must have had the right amount of room around them so you could move without bumping into corners. They are now pieces of furniture that sudden ruin has banished to a poky space, inadequate to its contents. You have to flatten yourself and look at your feet before stepping through. In plain sight, a partially oxidised picture frame surrounds that snapshot of Olivia with Marco in her arms, probably at the seaside, judging by their complexion. She was pointing towards the camera, Roberto must surely have been calling him, one eye closed, look at me look at me, while he flashed a milk-toothed smile, his hand gripping a little rubber dinosaur, a passion of his that lasted a few years.

'Don't go through there,' he says, intercepting my eyes on the assembled drapes. 'It's dangerous.'

I'd like to answer that I've no intention of doing so, but I can't push a syllable through my lips. He has banished the destruction to the other side, but it isn't completely separated; an unnatural sun shines through the fallen roof and lights up the back of the makeshift barrier. A breath of air from above stirs the hangings one after the other, and when the hem of the shorter one waves a little, I catch sight of the other side, of the rubble Marco has piled up just beyond.

On a shelf in the cooking area, a jar of anchovies survives. Olivia used to love them. The few remaining fillets levitate, suspended in the oil like tiny snakes darkened by time. She would have used them up in a matter of days, minced over a sliced tomato, in place of salt. She liked them like that, with garlic and lots of parsley. They could've been there for a hundred years and yet hurt me just as keenly.

Marco is sitting at the table, his arms crossed on the surface in front of him. The brown of his hair suddenly becomes the eye of a colourful vortex where the suspended anchovies, the ice bucket and surviving cups, the ethnic prints, the chilling neatness of the halved residual room all rotate in a furious spin. My weight converges towards my ankles, my blood drains from my head. I try to stop it, but it pays me no attention. The violent whirlwind slows in fits and starts, and the contrast of colours becomes undone in a milky whiteness. I'm falling into the whiteness, myself a bloodless white, and only when I'm about to touch it a shot of adrenaline returns me to my consciousness and to the blue of the sofa where Olivia slept her last living sleep, in my arms. I let myself lie down on it, I've felt this already, I know it will soon be over. Later, I hope that Marco hasn't noticed and so it is, his attention is elsewhere. I approach him cautiously.

'A penny for your thoughts,' I advance.

'I was wondering if we will have managed to get it sorted, for when I turn eighteen,' and he points all around. The doubt is reasonable, but I try to be supportive.

'Probably, there're still two years to go. Would you like to celebrate here?' I ask, fearful. Any word could be the wrong one.

'No, but I could live here, when I'm of age, couldn't I?'

'Of course you could, but who knows, you might want to go to uni in Rome, or somewhere else ...' I sit down too, but not facing him. I spread my hands on the table and find them much older than their body, especially the right one. The backs of my fingers are always stooped over my painting, it must have been that.

'Well, maybe, but this will always be my home, I can spend the summer here, and the Christmas holidays. I was thinking you and Granny could have me at weekends, though.'

Thankfully he isn't looking at me, he's still staring into the future ahead of him, a bit like a child would. A few tears mingle with my smile.

'Of course we'll have you stay, you're my only nephew, and Granny's only grandchild.' I am taking too much of a risk here, in this tragic room open to the sky. My voice cracks with repressed weeping. I regain control and start again: 'Perhaps in the meantime we might've been able to go back to our own homes, and you'll have to go to the village to see Granny.'

'That's true, I always forget that each one of us has their own home.'

'And they'll be yours one day,' I promise him.

'Why me? Don't you want a child of your own?' he asks, genuinely surprised.

'It's getting a little late for me, and I've yet to find a volunteer. I'd rather leave the flat to you.'

'I was never there very often, it was always you who came to us. You used to bring some sort of sweets, natural ones, you used to say. They were awful, you probably never even tried them. You liked them because they were natural, without colours and that, but what about the flavour? That matters too, you know? The good ones didn't taste of anything. I thought you were a bit mad.'

'And now?'

'Now I'm sure!' He laughs, shaking the curly ecosystem. A pause follows, natural, like the sweets.

'It must've been a big job here. It can't have been easy, on your own.'

'Rash helped me sometimes, and Andrea. And a couple of other friends came one Sunday.'

He knows what I must say. He arranges his face in resignation, hoping I won't take too long.

'Of course, you were working together. A small enterprise of minors, so if someone gets hurt ... I'm the one with the key and the responsibility ...'

'Don't go on, please. It's done now, there's nothing left to do. I'll wait for RE-CON-STRUC-TION.'

'You always let yourself off the hook with this story that *it's done now*. Things shouldn't happen *before* ... Before, you understand? Before they're done. They must not be *done*; they must *not happen*.' My throat dries up and I cough, spoiling the effect.

'Have you ever been young?' There it is, the strike under the belt.

'I don't remember,' I answer while I continue to cough, feeling a little ridiculous, and in fact he laughs, again.

'I'm sorry, I don't have any water, but there might be a beer in there. It won't be cool though.' He provokes me, taking advantage of my temporary weakness.

'Oh, leave it. I'll throw that away when we go,' I croak as soon as I can speak.

'They came to help me, I had to have something to give them, didn't I? What was I supposed to get? Fruit juice?' the fiend insists.

'Your grandmother still makes you juice at home, with fruit from the farmers' market. And you still drink it,' I protest with conviction.

'Let's leave Granny out of this now. Granny is out of bounds, she's a goddess,' he says, becoming serious again. I sigh and calm down. We stand up together, to leave. I look around at the anomalous room one last time, to store it in my memory.

'Can I help you in any way?' I ask without planning to.

'I don't think so ... actually, yes.' He lights up and opens a drawer. 'Can you tell me what the hell this thing is? I never saw Mum use it.' He pulls out a garlic press, one of the most useless gifts Olivia received when she got married, but no bride at that time would have dared exclude it from her gift list.

'I don't get you women,' he responds to the information. 'I always saw her crush garlic cloves with the flat of a knife. Grandma also does it like this,' and he mimes the action.

When we get back to the street, the first drops of the afternoon are falling from an overloaded sky. We're not surprised, it's a very wet spring.

'Look.' Marco stops halfway down an alleyway and points to the ground, next to a pipe. A large shrivelled rat lies, flat and light, among tall-stemmed weeds. In the profile of its head, unlike the rest of the carcass which seems to have been crushed from above, I can make out a tiny desiccated eye still betraying surprise and indignation at its death. I stand and stare at it, in spite of myself.

'Come on, it's raining.' Marco makes me jump, but it has actually already stopped. 'It must've starved to death,' he adds, hurrying away. 'There's nothing left in this town, not even for them.'

The way back, the same route as before, seems very short, as happens sometimes. When we sit in the car and look out, a thin layer of desert seems to have fallen on the windscreen with that bit of rain.

30

It happens now, in the years since the earthquake, that I wake up suddenly with the certainty of not having taken, last night, a pill essential to my survival. In the instants before realising that I don't take any form of medication, I ask myself if I still have time to swallow my pill or if I'm going to die. Perhaps it's the nightmare of the traumatised, perhaps the others have the same dreams. I could ask around here at the C.A.S.E., but I don't talk to the neighbours all that much. I don't talk much, anyway.

It's one of my best times, this one, when I wrap myself tighter in the warm blankets and reassure myself of my life. In the lucidity of awakening, I even face the earthquake, putting into perspective its wrong towards me. It did devastate us by killing Olivia, but in truth I was already unhappy before. I cannot sustain long-lasting wellbeing; I've always been looking for some fault or ailment to consume me. I need it, to feel that I exist. Incapable of happiness, I occasionally experience instants of unbearable grace.

If Olivia hadn't been stolen from us, that 6th April wouldn't have changed me much. It would've just given me an excuse, a cue for my natural inclinations. I'm immediately ashamed of my barely formulated thought, ashamed as I think of those who have lost someone. Orphans, widows and widowers, and mothers, whose loss lacks even a word in the dictionary daring to name their conditions.

And now my mother and Lorenza come to mind, the inventory of seasons they've spent a few tombstones away from each other, entwining themselves in the same loss, day after day, out of necessity.

I met her last Sunday downstairs, Lorenza. I hadn't seen her for a week. She was walking her little dog, Antonio's gift, around the platforms. Bric doesn't like it, he growls quietly at it sometimes, jealous, as if to say that he can't stand it but knows he can't bite it. She seemed a little less skinny. Instead of the usual black from head to toe, she was wearing a white top over dark trousers. She smiled at me, and touched my arm with the hand not holding the lead.

'Hasn't your mother told you the good news?' she asked before the quadruped pulled her away. She turned, still smiling, to see me shake my head, before our slightly mad neighbour sneaked up on me dressed in a multitude of colours, to spoil the surprise.

'You know she's pregnant? Her husband's put a bun in her oven, hee hee hee!' she enlightened me, her Ss and bad breath hissing through the few remaining teeth. 'They'll be off to a proper house soon, before the baby comes.'

I pretended I had to rush to the toilet and ran upstairs, while she gnawed away at the tail of her bit of gossip. My mother was sitting in her armchair, her bony fingers spread on her kitchen apron. No cooking smells from the kitchen, not yet. She looked at me just a moment, until she understood that I knew, and was concerned for her. I had thought she'd been behaving oddly for a bit, as if fixating on something.

'I was waiting for the right time to tell you. It's great news. Of course, I'll miss her, Lorenza.' She uttered the name slowly enough to remember, in the meantime, the affection they have shared.

'Anyway, we'll move away from here too, when our homes have been repaired. You'll keep in touch, won't you?' I tentatively suggested to the one who hadn't wanted to get close to the impermanent neighbours.

'Yes, we are planning to. She'll come and see us and we'll always meet at the cemetery. It won't be the same as having her in the next platform, but it isn't important. The important thing is that a baby will be born, a salvation. The Holy Mother has answered my prayers, I have prayed for this, every night.' It sounded like something she had repeatedly told herself.

'I thought, thin as she was, that she wouldn't be able to get pregnant ...'

'She started having periods again a few months ago, she'd tried so hard to put a little weight back on,' she went on to explain, her voice and hands light in the air. She was becoming animated by the pride that stirs people when they talk about their own children. 'She hadn't realised at first, she thought her cycle was still irregular. Just imagine, Antonio had just given her the dog, to keep her company, when they found out she was pregnant.'

I felt a sudden sharp wound, hearing her so well informed about Lorenza's periods and so ignorant of mine, gone with Olivia. It's true that I have never talked to her about it, but is it possible that she's never noticed the sanitary pad packet in the bathroom is always sealed, always the same? She must surely have known and not said anything, as I haven't.

'I think you'd better get ready to be Granny. Antonio's mother is gone too; this baby will need a grandmother.'

'I'd be happy to, of course. We've looked up the bus times, there's one stopping just a few minutes away from the house they're moving to. I could go on that, and help her out. A baby needs a lot of time, and she truly has no one. But we'll have to see. When people move away it's easy to lose contact.'

'I don't think it'll be the case with you two,' I immediately reassured her. She wasn't listening, a smile was starting to light up her face, while bit by bit, the afternoon pulled away from the room.

'She said she wants me to be the baby's godmother. I've told her not to talk about this sort of thing yet, for good luck, it's too early. She's only in her third month.' She had been clearly gratified by the request.

It's so quiet, tonight. The dog that always barks in the distance is now sleeping, and Bric isn't whimpering softly in his dreams. Not even the usual mystery cough can be heard, perhaps it's been cured, in the end. Some days it's already hot in the middle of the day, before the rain comes. I turn over in bed and change the subject. I think of all the written and oral tests that Marco still has to get through, if he wants to pass the year with just a few re-sits in September, and for a moment I think of Sandro; if he doesn't hurry up and come back I'll forget him.

Then a sound reaches me from the outside, at first I think I must have got it wrong. For long moments, nothing more, as if teasing, almost. I try to find a position that leaves both my ears uncovered, and I tune them to the darkness beyond the window. I can feel the microscopic creaking of cartilage as it responds to the intermittent stimulus, but that may only be my imagination. Again, perhaps, then nothing, like a game of auditory hide and seek. I get up and reach the balcony on bare feet, careful to avoid the booby-trap of Marco's shoes. I go out, holding my breath, hopeful. The line of trees I sense down the road, clad in new, tender, soft-green foliage, even they seem to be waiting. Finally, there it is. *Kew*, calls the scops owl, *kew, kew, kew, kew*. Its call is an E flat major, Roberto told us that time on the terrace, and to demonstrate he had run inside, to the piano, and pressed the corresponding key.

'It's true, it's exactly the same!' Olivia had enthusiastically confirmed, smiling at him, tossing back her hair in the light of the lamp, in a room of their first home together. And so he went on playing one note after each call, and the duet continued until the bird lost interest. We had fun, and Olivia handed him a glass of something good to drink, when she still believed in their future together.

Kew, repeats the nocturnal singer, *kew, kew, kew, kew*. It's taken a long break, since the moment before the earthquake, but I am not at all distressed to hear it now, after that. It must be perched in one of the two linden trees across the way, the sounds gracefully produced by its tiny throat ringing in the still, sparkling air. The stars can hear it, so bright after the usual afternoon storm, and the invisible new moon, perhaps even the sleepless man in the platform across can hear it, behind the curtainless window always lit at this time of night. There is a sort of hope in the note, and I find myself a little pathetic in the act of accepting it.

Roberto asks what has happened instead of saying hello. I point the phone towards the linden tree and pray for the *kew* not to stop just now. But it isn't the sort to show me up, it seems to want to give the best of itself in these few instants, as if in an audition. It seems closer, louder. Roberto is laughing into the phone, when I put it back to my ear.

'Did you get that?' I ask, a little worried I might have scared him, at two in the morning.

'Yes, loud and clear. The scops owl's solo. It's been years since I last heard it.' He seems happy with this sort of prank.

'Are you still scared?'

'No, that went when I understood that it wasn't my son's aunt calling me, but the screwball from a long time ago. Do you remember the note your friend is singing?'

'Flat E major, maestro.'

'Well done. Did Marco hear it?' he asks, almost moved, like any dad anxious to show the details of the world to his own child.

'If I tried to wake up your son for something like this, he'd chuck the first shoe he can lay his hands on at my head. You should know how romantic he is,' is my matter-of-fact reply. I find myself in a sudden hurry to hang up.

I gave in to an insidious and fleeting temptation, the desire to reawaken, for an instant, the youths we were for a long time, in the last millennium. I replayed a familiarity belonging to what seems a prehistoric age, seen from the here and now. But getting closer to the father, beyond the bare minimum essential for Marco's welfare, soon upsets me. Roberto is what he is, he's always been like that. And I have stopped forgiving him, just like my mother has.

Yesterday he was the one to call me.

'Has Marco told you that he'll follow me on tour this summer? He'll be my page turner; he wants to earn a bit of money. I hope he'll reconnect with music a little.'

They haven't been able to share even that, not quite. When Roberto left home, his son refused to keep up his piano lessons. He does occasionally torture an electric guitar in Rash's garage. Rash batters the drums, and another friend on the bass completes the trio. But it isn't a real passion, I only know about it because from time to time he asks for money to replace broken chords.

'No, he didn't tell me anything ... how long for?'

'I don't know, that depends on school and how many re-sits he'll have to prepare for. Anyway, his plan is to visit the cities where I'm going to play, I think it's a good idea.'

'Of course it's a good idea ...' I replied from the balcony, turning towards the quiet interior where my mother was trimming artichokes, unaware of yet another departure. I could see her in the months to come, sitting on the sweltering sofa, the network of her veins standing under the thin skin of her legs, the hands of the clock on the wall in front caught in their meaningless rounds.

31

The second woman is screaming too. This time I've carved out her mouth from the start, and she started to vent right away, while I was still working on her. My friend Mariano, master maker of ceramic whistles, guided me over the phone on how to turn her into a whistling instrument. Now she's a hollow doll, and by blowing into one of the two holes in her left hand, you get a sound. I have never been so anxious when opening the kiln, I was swallowing saliva as I turned the handle. I was worried about how the clay would hold during the bisque firing, and how the colours would turn out after the stoneware firing, especially the copper green and manganese brown, you never know what they'll look like in the end, when you're applying the black pigment to the bisque.

I'm pleased with her: with her open arms and the slight forward tilt of her torso she looks very much like her twin, born a few days ago here in the workshop. Her dress is simpler, sleeveless, of coarse plain-coloured wool, thankfully the copper green didn't let me down. I've carved a thin motif just above the hem, only a thin point, to embellish it a little. Again her feet are imprisoned, but in a slightly undulating plane, where I have made some holes, to surprise her. I have in fact fired something else along with the woman, something she could not see – I turned her back on purpose. Only in the end she watched me mount the bees and butterflies on metal wire, with all the flowers I have modelled for her. I planted them all around her, fixing the metallic stems with a drop of glue in the small holes in the base. Now she's surrounded by multi-coloured petals, wings, flight. Her expression is suddenly new, she continues to shout but she's overwhelmed by beauty, and her cry is one of wonder, of protest, still, and perhaps of joy.

In rapid succession, I touch the wires with my fingertips. They vibrate like the chords of a harp and the hard petals collide against each other, producing a different sound. She listens with me, above her own spring-time.

First thing this morning, I put the screaming twins on the old table pushed against the outside wall of the house, to check from time to time that they're shining in the sun, and not fighting. It's too bright a day to keep it at a distance, so I've come outside myself with everything I need, and I've gone back to my regular work. Party favours for a wedding, 120 breakfast bowls with respective saucers, large enough to place a brioche or a handful of biscuits next to the milk. The bride has chosen various designs, but prefers decorations with grapes or pomegranates, they bring good luck, she says. She has requested that all fruits are opened up, the red grains inside quite visible, perhaps some of them rolling away. I told her not to worry, the grains will be sparkling in all their splendour.

'How will you make them sparkle?' she asked, surprised.

'It isn't difficult, just a touch of white in the red,' and I showed her a jug with a similar design. She decided to double the number of pomegranates, at the expense of the oranges.

Some of the pieces are already dry, and I reward myself with a cigarette and a bit of a rest. Better have an apple first, so I can tell my mother I've had lunch when she calls me at three, as usual. Sitting on the wooden bench by the door to the workshop, I smoke with half-closed eyes, following through my lashes the comings and goings of a swallow busy feeding her brood. I saw them yesterday, their chirping throats and soft beaks open wide, waiting for the return of their mother. I am distracted by the furry buzzing of a bumble-bee; I hadn't seen any yet this year. Picking from the infinite possibilities at its disposal, it decides to land on one of the flowers around the sculpture, but it finds no pollen to suck inside the ceramic calyx and immediately flies off, in search of real sweetness. Who knows how far the insect can see, if it's aware of the clouds rising so fast and filling with water. It'll have to take refuge from the storm, a single drop could squash it, if it comes down hard from Mount Sirente like the other times. I take everything back inside before the rain. On the telephone, my mother tells me that it has just started there, they had their lunch a little while ago and Marco's already studying literature for tomorrow's test. I'm not sure about that one, he's been behaving for a few days now. When there's silence in the children's room, it means they're up to something.

As for her, though, I don't need to ask. She'll be sitting in her armchair, knitting, like any other grandmother, a minuscule red jumper with white Christmas stars – that's when the baby's due and in any case she can't risk blue or pink, although the signs point to a boy for Lorenza, this time.

'It would be best,' my mother maintained yesterday. 'A little girl would remind her too much of the child who's no longer there.' She speaks of nothing else now. She regularly cooks for the pregnant woman and, she might just as well, for Antonio too, as his wife really can't manage and he works, poor man. He does the washing up though, always. I should think so, I feel like saying but don't; I'd like to see us having to take care of that, too. There is much coming and going of covered containers between the two platforms, full of hot food, better tolerated by Lorenza. Marco also undertakes carrier duties with benign forbearance, and I too, of course.

But I do get a little impatient from time to time, up and down those stairs.

I leave the door open on the cloudburst and stand looking out. Apart from a few rumblings in the distance, no dog-scaring thunder today, but the drops fall violently, like slivers of sky, they almost go through the plants. They bounce off the car, forming a cloud of mist over the bonnet. The rain makes runnels down the slight slope on one side of the drive, and is soon flowing into a short murky stream before dispersing into the countryside. It drags into little whirlpools fragments torn from trees, leaves, twigs, soaked flowers. The bumble-bee must've been quick to find shelter, in the hollow of a tree, under a gutter, a guest of the bees in their colourful homes around the bend over there, or perhaps it's indoors, silent and still, waiting for it to be over. I've put the twins by the closed window, so they too can watch the downpour.

I lie down on the sofa, listening, having ensured there are no fresh stains on me. As the minutes pass, my attention slackens, as does the racket outside, and I fall into a shallow doze, broken by the occasional start. Only my sense of smell remains alert at the back of my awareness, so full are my nostrils with dampened dust, soaked earth and the essence of everything around, heightened by the rain and the wind. At times I may perceive, with a flicker of residual discernment, a scent different from the everyday ones I'm used to, but it still doesn't warrant opening my eyes, not even when it seems to be approaching, insistent. The vetiver hand lands on my cheek, and immediately after moves to my hair, stroking from the roots to the end of its medium length. Moving it away from my face. There's a pause, an instant. It doesn't frighten me; I know I am being watched. I keep my eyes closed, perhaps I smile, and then fingers caress my lips, then other lips.

'You taste of apple,' a low voice says.

'I ate one not long ago. Have you seen a bumble-bee, by any chance? I'm worried about it,' I whisper to his face, so close. I can see him now, in the half-light, one knee on the brick floor.

'Are you not worried about me, coming from afar under this deluge?' He pretends to take offence.

Now I touch his hair, a few grey strands, barely damp. I make room for him and he lies down next to me, putting his arms around me.

'You're big, you're not scared.'

'I'm jealous of this bumble-bee. Who is it? A relative of the hornet?'

'A cousin, I believe.' We shift a little to fit around each other in the available space.

'It's full of novelties here. Who are those two screaming at the window? Are you the woman among the flowers?'

'Oh, those. My attempts at sculpture. I made them for fun, they're not for sale.'

He smiles and watches my mouth closely while I speak. But there isn't enough distance between us to be able to see each other properly. He shivers, but not with the cold, and holds me a little tighter.

'Have you been here long?' I ask, stroking his cheekbone with the back of my index finger.

'Long enough to watch you sleep with the door open, beautiful and careless.'

'We're in the countryside, you forget. You can leave the door open, especially if you're expecting someone.'

'Liar, I never come mid-week ...' he rebuts, while the hard shape of his sex starts to gently push against my clothed belly.

'I didn't say I was waiting for you,' I whisper in his ear, but he's no longer listening to me and doesn't answer, his body proving mine wrong.

Later in the afternoon a heart-warming blue regains the sky, and I suggest a stroll. We walk almost unsteady on our legs, still wobbly after love. Keeping a promise, I show him the dog-rose bushes overflowing with flowers. The water drips on the grass from petals and thorns, from the tips of leaves, under a feverish orange sunset. We stop to admire the last exuberant instants of the sun, then its passing beyond the mountain. I receive another kiss, just for this. We get back towards the house in the suddenly cold air, with muddy shoes and a full heart.

Sandro invites me out to dinner, and I ask him why he didn't get bread from San Gregorio today.

'I was in a hurry, I was afraid I wouldn't find you,' he says, serious, his hand resting on my car. I'm about to set off, I must go and change.

'Why didn't you ever call me?' I reproach him harshly, turning the engine off.

'I tried to resist you, from a distance. Then I gave up and broke all the speed limits on my way back. Come.' He points at the house with a slight rotation of his head. He opens the car door and pulls me gently by an arm.

'Not before a shower, I'm starting to feel uncomfortable.' He suddenly pulls his middle-aged neck away from my fingers reaching to caress it, as if it were a weak point not to be displayed.

'I'll let you go then, but we'll sleep together later. And don't forget the red pumps.'

In the mirror my body has already changed. The shoulders have straightened up, lifting breasts I'd forgotten I had, and the curve of my buttocks is highlighted under the hand rubbing on lotion. There is no real need for it, my skin is already smoother just for the persisting effect of human touch, but I want to use it anyway, and I look for the underwear set I once got as a present and have never worn. I find it at the bottom of the drawer, the labels still attached. For my hair, I steal a little product from my nephew, and decide to do without stockings – it is June, after all. The flower-print dress crosses over my breasts and the belt ties up in a bow at the waist, then drops down to the knee to peep at the ballet pumps. I say goodbye to my mother and nephew; I have already told them I'll stay at Silvia's tonight.

'Where are you going, all dolled up?' Marco asks.

'To dinner, with a man. He's downstairs already.'

They both make a dash for the balcony, bumping into each other in the rush. Bric barks behind them and tries to slip in between. He yelps, Granny has accidentally stepped on him. I don't think they can hear me laughing on my way downstairs.

Sandro has come out of the car, he's observing the C.A.S.E. The crazy woman is keeping a close eye on him, half hidden behind a parked van; later he'll tell me that she even asked him who he was waiting for, and he answered Caterina. I twirl on my toes to let myself be admired by everyone watching, the skirt of my dress flaring up into a wheel. As we drive off, I turn for an instant towards Marco above, the dog in his arms; it wasn't fair on him to miss seeing his aunt go out with a much older someone.

At the restaurant, I ignore the complicit look from the waiter, perhaps accustomed to the professor dining in the company of other women. After the starter and the truffle *tagliatelle*, we look at each other and I recognise a wistfulness for the two of us alone. So we forget our hunger for anything else and we leave.

The window in the bedroom I once vacuumed is now a picture of stars. The most important named; none can be bothered to fall for the benefit of our wishes, and so the repertoire of lovers' banalities is finally exhausted. Sandro slides my shoes off and pulls the bow at my waist. My body welcomes him again, with a small moan.

32

Marco is ready to leave. He has packed a sports bag with his summer clothes and a rucksack with the books of the two subjects he has to revise for September. He, Rash and Andrea, the boy who lives in the M.A.P., celebrated not failing the year outright by getting blind drunk the other night. At three in the morning he called me to pick them up from the town centre. Bring me a clean T-shirt, he said.

Piazza Regina Margherita had been taken over by young ones with beers or iced cocktails in their hands, sitting at the tables of the various local bars, which only open in the summer and dispense alcohol and really loud music. Many were standing around, some leaning back against the plaster façades of the buildings. They were sipping from fogged glasses, nodding their heads to the music, and I had to zig-zag among them to avoid the obstacles of their indifferent bodies. After a few dozen metres, along Via Garibaldi, silence unfolded, barely wounded by the booming of the bass and a whiff of dried piss in a corner. I wonder how it comes that everybody decides to urinate in the same place.

Marco and Andrea had concealed themselves in a recessed doorway, Rash was no longer with them. On the cobblestones nearby, undigested food had been sicked up, a halo of sprays around it. My nephew had recovered a little, or perhaps he hadn't drunk as much. On his chest the white cotton was dotted with regurgitated reddish clumps. He guessed my question and reassured me, it wasn't blood but the strawberries they'd had at Rash's after dinner. He immediately changed T-shirts, making sure to keep the dirty one away from his face, quite alert by now. The other had thrown himself on the step, his head lolling back against the wood. His clammy greyish pallor shone in the half-light, and a hand seemed to have roughly smoothed back his hair, Marco's, I guessed. He slept the chemical sleep of drunks, the cyclic recurring of his rolling eyes visible in the thin gap between the eyelids.

I went back to the square to get a coffee for Andrea and found them again, just as I had left them. The more alert one gently put the plastic cup to his friend's lips, after a quick sip to test its temperature. He pulled him up, holding the back of his head. A mother couldn't have been more attentive. Then a few gulps of water, he washed his face with the rest. They weren't the gestures of someone who's drunk, they were slow and tender. I observed them appreciatively, wondering where, when, whom he had learned them from. I found an answer for myself.

Andrea cooperated feebly to finding his own feet. We moved away with difficulty, offering him support, me on one side and Marco on the other. He seemed to fall asleep again at times, he'd drag his feet and become a dead weight. In the square, the discarded bottles on the ground would roll about if we accidentally nudged them in passing, the few bins by now overflowing with empties. We stopped for a quick rest, leaning against the ancient dust of an abandoned store window. At the Bright Fountain we more or less dropped Andrea on a step and I went to get the car. He slept some more on the back seat, on the way home. Marco turned around to wake him when we got close to the M.A.P. and slipped him a chewing gum.

'It's for his breath,' said the expert. At four in the morning, Andrea acted out for us the famous scene of the drunkard trying to find the keyhole with his key. Marco was laughing and running a commentary under his breath, he barely stopped himself from helping. We left after the door silently closed behind him. I wasn't in the mood for scolding on the way back and we didn't exchange a single word. We were thinking about Andrea, fearing for him on account of his father.

My nephew has spent the last three days persuading Bric that he can't take him to Rome. He repeats the same reasons, until the very last minute.

'You'd end up staying at home by yourself, especially at night when we're at the concerts,' he replies to the other's imaginary objections. 'It is true that there's a park nearby where you could run around, but who will I leave you with if we have to go away?'

The dog pricks up his ears and looks at him questioningly. Finding his master lying down on the rug on his tummy, he delivers a lick over his dried-up spots.

'There's no Lorenza in Rome, to look after you when these two go and see the family, people hardly give each other the time of day over there. There's Irene on the third floor, but I really doubt her mother … they have a cat, anyway.' He strokes him, and raising his fur he checks a wound on the dog's back, which Bric received when he got into a fight with a bigger dog last week.

'And I'll come and see you over the next few months, two or three times at least. And at the end of August I have my exam, and then I won't go away again. Time will just zip by.'

His grandmother has stopped in her tracks, her marble hands in the air. She listens avidly to the last few sentences, without bothering to conceal her interest. She's wrapping the apple tart, still warm, in some white paper, that's the last noise in the flat while we wait for Roberto to come and collect his son. We look at each other for a moment, she and

I, a single happy tear moistening the depth of a wrinkle. Our boy will come back, at least for another school year. So it seems, at the beginning of summer.

My mother starts again to fold the paper, the same crackling noise that sounded almost painful earlier now feeling quite pleasant. She applies adhesive tape to the right spots, methodically. She has also prepared a case of jars sterilised in boiling water, containing Marco's favourite tomato sauces, basil, *arrabbiata*, peppers and olives. The strawberry jam's there too, two jars of it, sweet and sour vegetable pickles, and a generous serving of chicken stew prepared last night. It only needs to be reheated, on a low heat in a saucepan, she reminds the one who put a cup of milk directly on the lit stove a couple of years ago.

A message reaches my pocket. I read it almost without surprise; he writes from a service station on the Adriatic motorway. It's only halfway through the ten days' break he had planned. A rambling message concluding that he needs to get away for a bit, he's too taken with me, he says. Some of the text is missing. I shove it back where it was, next to a moderate, secondary rage. It will smart, but later.

I can't deal with it now, Roberto's already ringing the bell, he's downstairs, under the platform. Let's go down, Marco urges. He carries the bag and rucksack, Granny the cake and I the case with provisions, Bric only his own bewilderment. The ever-present neighbour, looking very flowery today, waits behind the creaking hinges and follows us towards the car park, singing to herself *L'Aquila bella mia*, as usual. We follow Marco's extra-long legs, they seem bandy beneath his Bermuda shorts, but it's only the effect of his thinness. He has bought himself a pair of blue jeans, dark and with no rips, for his father's concerts.

'What are you going to wear with them?' I asked him.

'A white shirt, or a blue one.' Far too smart for him.

'Won't you come upstairs for a coffee, before setting off again?' I ask Roberto after we've loaded his boot. No, there is no time, he's playing in Nettuno tonight and Marco will start turning pages.

Our nephew bends down to kiss us, holding back his hair so as not to sting our eyes. He says goodbye to Bric and leaves him in my arms, like he did when he went on the school trip, but the dog jumps down as soon as he hears the engine and runs off in pursuit. He chases the whirlwind of exhaust with all the desperate energy of his short legs and mongrel's heart, his black fur shining in the sun. Marco leans out of the window to look at him, then appears agitated inside the vehicle. Bric increases the pace of his mad chase, he will not resign himself to losing another. But he's no longer young, nor a hound, he stumbles and starts to fall back, tired, the unjust speed of the vehicle is leaving him behind. The gap between them begins to grow and his hope gives way. We see him disappear behind a bush, perhaps he's thrown himself down on the ground, to catch his breath. We wait for him a little, while a pollen-laden wind starts to blow.

A vibration announces the message completing itself. I turn to read it in the shadow of my body. He'll come back, he asks me to wait for him. A long kiss. I put it back in my pocket, to decant.

'I hope he'll eat, in Rome ...' my mother sighs. We go back inside, leaving the doorway open for Bric.

'He certainly won't starve, with all that food you made him,' I observe while I get the post and start leafing through the bills. 'You could've chosen larger jars, though, they were all single-portion and there will be two of them at the table.'

Already on the stairs, she stops and turns towards me without answering, her lips contracted, a halo of dark rays carved into the skin. From somewhere comes the noise of a window slammed by the wind. The painful summary of her life pulls her cotton-clad shoulder, outlines the rigid fold of her bare elbow. On the banister, worn by the harshness of the world, her wedding band still shines.

Acknowledgements

Thank you to Raffaella Lops, for all the troubles you have caused me. They were indispensable for the completion of this book. Thank you to Giorgio Bafile, Danilo Bandini, Antonio Camorchia, Paolo Catone, Mario Cavalieri, Franca Cetra, Luigi Di Paolo, Mauro Di Pietrantonio, Francesco Di Simone, Vittoria Esquilino, Anna Filipponi, Mariano Fuga, Laura Grignoli, Tiziana Irti, Adelaide Leone, Carla and Roberto Manilla, Annangela Maroder, Sara Palumbo, Diego Pompei, Fausto Roncone, Enrico Santangelo, Gianfranco Scaramella. Each one of them will remember why. Thank you to Loretta Santini who still believes in me, and all the women at Elliot, in particular Patrizia Renzi who rescues me even in my dreams. To Marzia Grillo, for her precision and patience. To Paolo G., G as in generous. To Kylee Doust, for her professionalism and congeniality. Thank you to Tommaso for Bric and to Giacomo for the computer, and to both of you for patiently bearing with me. If I have forgotten anyone, I thank them and apologise.

About the author

Donatella Di Pietrantonio was born and grew up in Arsita, a small village in the province of Teramo, and now lives in Penne where she practises as a paediatric dentist. From the age of nine she has been writing stories, fables, poems, and now novels. *My Mother Is a River*, her first novel, was first published in Italy in 2011, where it won the Tropea and the John Fante literary prizes. Her second book, *Bella Mia*, was published in 2014. It won the Brancati Prize and was shortlisted for the prestigious Strega Literary Prize in 2014. Both *My Mother Is a River* and *Bella Mia* have been translated into German.

Also available from Calisi Press

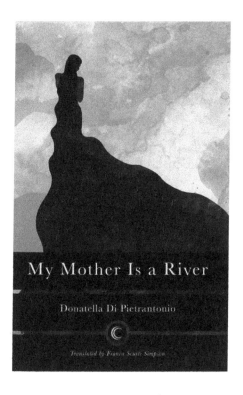

The sensitive and powerful story of the love between a mother and her daughter, a love "gone wrong from the start".

A surprising new novel, revealing a strong voice weaving a compelling magic spell.

www.calisipress.com